SOMNAMBULISM, SLEEPWALKING AND SECRETS IN VICTORIAN LITERATURE

Zainab Ayoub

authorHOUSE®

AuthorHouse™ UK
1663 Liberty Drive
Bloomington, IN 47403 USA
www.authorhouse.co.uk
Phone: 0800 047 8203 (Domestic TFN)
 +44 1908 723714 (International)

© 2019 Zainab Ayoub. All rights reserved.

No part of this book may be reproduced, stored in a retrieval system, or transmitted by any means without the written permission of the author.

Published by AuthorHouse 06/20/2019

ISBN: 978-1-7283-8994-3 (sc)
ISBN: 978-1-7283-8993-6 (e)

Print information available on the last page.

Any people depicted in stock imagery provided by Getty Images are models, and such images are being used for illustrative purposes only.
Certain stock imagery © Getty Images.

This book is printed on acid-free paper.

Because of the dynamic nature of the Internet, any web addresses or links contained in this book may have changed since publication and may no longer be valid. The views expressed in this work are solely those of the author and do not necessarily reflect the views of the publisher, and the publisher hereby disclaims any responsibility for them.

Contents

Introduction vii

"My dear John's Murdered! I did it in My Sleep": Sleepwalking & Women 1

'Who is he, this Invisible being that rules me?' Sleepwalking / The Gothic/ The Supernatural 29

'Britain is Sleepwalking into Hell's Pit' Sleepwalking & the State 47

Conclusion 59
Bibliography 61

Introduction

Sleepwalking is a convoluted subject which has aroused much research since the nineteenth century. What did sleepwalking mean to the Victorians? Was it a form of insanity? Or was it a physical act of another state of consciousness? Mesmerism, or animal magnetism, had made its original impact in pre-revolutionary France; when Franz Anton Mesmer arrived from Vienna in 1778 and published *Sur La Decouverte du Magnestise Animal* in 1779. Mesmerism was considered as a type of cure for physical and psychic ills. After its introduction in Britain in the 1830's, it was used to support widely differing theories of the self and reality.

The nineteenth century was an era of change and innovation. It was also a period of instability whereby the Victorian period, especially the *fin de siècle* witnessed the emergence of the New Woman, an awareness of homosexuality and an increase in divorce.[1] The title of this thesis: 'Me/Myself/I' reflects the instability and anxiety of identity in the nineteenth century. As the title suggests, this dissertation is concerned with change, transgression of boundaries, transition from one identity to another and the instability of the self, society and the state.

The texts utilised in chapter one are George Eliot's *The Mill on the Floss* (1860), Thomas Hardy's *Tess of the d'Urbervilles* (1891) and Wilkie Collins' *The Moonstone* (1868), *The Law and the Lady* (1875) and "Who Killed Zebedee?" (1881). These novels address important themes relating to marriage, law, the status of women and the self. What links these texts together is that they focus on individual concern about the self, within a

---

[1] Jenny Bourne Taylor, and Sally Shuttleworth, ed. *Embodied Selves: An Anthology of Psychological Texts 1830-1890* (Oxford: Clarendon Press, 1998), p.179.

society which seeks to control men and women, rather than conform to new ways of thinking. Sleepwalking in these novels is significant because it is presented to the reader as a form of escapism, whereby two states of consciousness merge to form an identity, an identity, which would be unacceptable in normal day-to-day society.

In chapter two, sleepwalking is discussed in relation to Joseph Sheridan Le Fanu "Carmilla" (1872), Guy de Maupassant's "Le Horla" (1887) and Bram Stoker's *Dracula* (1897). In "Carmilla" and *Dracula*, sleepwalking is used as a medium to express familial volatility and an anxiety about women, sex and sexuality. In "Le Horla", sleepwalking is used to depict the narrator's disintegrating mind, in the face of a supernatural being.

Sleepwalking in the final chapter extends beyond the bedroom. In this chapter is used as a metaphor to represent the decline of Britain as an imperial power. Sleepwalking is discussed in relation to Robert Wiene's film *The Cabinet of Dr. Caligari* (1919), which depicts the hypnotic control that the German authority has over the individual. Gustave Le Bon extends this image of leader as hypnotist to portray his concern over the power the leader/crowd has in determining the future of France in *Crowd Psychology* (1895).

The aim of this dissertation is to argue that sleepwalking is not simple acts which take place, but sleepwalking affects nearly every facet of life. The significance of sleepwalking is that it highlights the instability and anxiety about many aspects of life such as: the safety of the home, gender subject-positions, sex, sexuality, criminal/marital laws, society's double standards, the state, and questions the notion of a stable identity.

Before one begins to discuss the significance of sleepwalking, it is worth explaining what sleepwalking meant to the Victorians. Sleepwalking in the Victorian epoch was essential in understanding the complexity of the mind. Jenny Bourne Taylor states:

> The relationship between the conscious and the unconscious mind and the significance and workings of memory were central to the debate about the nature of individual and social identity[2]

---

[2] J.B.Bullen, ed. *Writing and Victorianism* (London: Longman, 1997), p.140. All further references to this text are given parenthetically in the dissertation.

The prevailing conception of the unconscious in Victorian England was 'known as the unconscious proper', in which the process of repression was absolutely inaccessible. Thus, the language of the repressed would be spoken vis-à-vis the medium of dreams, which in some cases lead to sleepwalking. Michel Foucault stressed this danger in his well known critique of crude notions of Victorian sexual repression, in the first volume of the *History of Sexuality*. Foucault argued that it was during the nineteenth century that identity surfaced from a secret self, produced by repression, hidden beneath the visible identity which functioned in a moral society.

In Charles Dickens' *Oliver Twist*, the discourse of sleepwalking at the time Dickens was writing was at its peak. Early in the novel, Oliver is described as:

> Having roused himself from sleep, he was not thoroughly awake. There is a drowsy state, between sleeping and waking, when you dream more in five minutes with your eyes half open, and yourself half conscious of everything that is passing around you, than you would in five nights with your eyes fast closed and senses wrapt in perfect unconsciousness. At such times, a mortal knows just enough of what his mind is doing, to form some conception of its mighty powers[3]

Oliver's hovering between the sleep and wake state in the example cited and again later in the novel when he sees, in a half dream Fagin and Monks 'peering in at him through Mrs. Maylie's window' (p.212), serve to underline and express Oliver's lack of autonomy; which is mirrored in his disordered state of falling asleep and being awake at the same time. The depiction of Oliver's half sleeping state is important because it allows the reader insight into Oliver's mind as a way of understanding his consciousness. The argument that is endorsed in this thesis is that sleepwalking is not simply the physical act of walking with eyes open; it is a way in which the somnambulist can re-enact his suppressed thoughts.

Freud shared with his predecessors the belief that there is something about the dreaming mind that differs radically from the mind in its waking state:

---

[3] Charles Dickens, *Oliver Twist* (London: Harmondsworth, 1985), p.106.

> It is not that [the dream state] is more negligent, more unreasonable more forgetful, more incomplete say than waking thoughts; it is qualitatively different from it and so at first not comparable to it, it does not think, calculate, judge at all. Dreams are nothing other than a peculiar form of thinking made possible by the conditions of the state of sleep[4]

Freud's theories of repressed psychology were drawn upon Victorian theorists such as William Hamilton, who argued in his lectures on metaphysics given during the 1830's and 40's, that the unconscious plays a central role in all mental and physical activity. Hamilton's theory was taken up by many writers particularly Eneas Sweetland Dallas who aimed, in *The Gay Science* (1866), to develop a 'science in the laws of pleasure' based on the unconscious otherwise known as the 'hidden soul'. The relevance of this background information is to show a scientific awareness of the time that Collins, Hardy, George Eliot, Le Fanu, Stoker, Maupassant were writing in, and what sleepwalking meant to their contemporaries.

---

[4] Helen Small and Trudi Tate, ed. *Literature, Science, Psychoanalysis 1830-1970* (Oxford: Oxford University Press, 2003), p.131/132

"My dear John's Murdered! I did it in My Sleep": Sleepwalking & Women

The Victorian bourgeoisie, as Michel Foucault observed, defined its sexuality in contrast to that of earlier periods as being 'subjected to a regime so intense as to represent a constant danger'[5]. Foucault's view is true. In Thomas Hardy's *Tess of the d'Urbervilles*, George Eliot's *The Mill on the Floss*, Wilkie Collins' *The Moonstone; The Law and the Lady* and "Who Killed Zebedee?" women are violated in some form and are expected to be silent. In *The Moonstone*, Rachel's diamond, a symbol of her virginity, is taken away by Franklin Blake. Tess is raped and it is she, not Alec, who feels ashamed. Similarly, Maggie is expected to suffer the consequences of Stephen Guest's behaviour as well as her own, after they elope. Eustace adopts an alias surname in order to marry Valeria and separates from her because she wants to prove his innocence; Priscilla likewise is deserted by Zebedee prior to their wedding day and is expected to keep quiet about it. It is clear from these examples that women are not only abused, but they have to deal with the brunt of men's conduct. John Ruskin wrote that:

> The home is the place of peace; the shelter, not only from injury, but from all terror, doubt and division[6]

---

[5] Michel Foucault, *The History of Sexuality*, Vol. 1, trans. Robert Hurley (New York: Vintage, 1980), p.128.
[6] John Ruskin, *Sesame and Lilies: Two Lectures* (London: George Allen, 1901), p.39. All further references to this text are given parenthetically in the dissertation.

These five texts question Ruskin's claims that the home is a place of 'shelter'. If anything, the home is a place of chaos and restriction, where female characters attempt to transgress. Sleepwalking is an important aspect in each of these novels because it highlights the problem with society and the anxiety about society's morals within the home and family. Thus, the depiction of sleepwalking undermines any sense of stability, because society forces men and women to adopt rigid social roles that characters cannot escape and have to suffer the consequences in the event they choose to reject them.

E.S Dallas stated in *The Gay Science* that:

> We have such a fairy in our thoughts, a willing and tricksy worker which commonly bears the name of Imagination, and which may be named- as I think more clearly- the Hidden Soul[7]

The 'hidden soul' is the central preoccupation in Collins' *The Moonstone*. Throughout the whole novel, what is conscious and unconscious intertwine in order to create a detective story. Franklin Blake, Rachel Verinder, Rosanna Spearman, Godfrey Ablewhite and Ezra Jennings, conceal information about the moonstone or themselves. In other words, this novel is concerned with the individual's consciousness and appearances. To be more specific, this text is not simply about understanding the individual per se, but it is about the status of women and how they are vulnerable to self destruction because they are expected to follow social convention. What is significant in this text and in Hardy's *Tess of the d'Urbervilles* is that Franklin Blake and Angel Clare are the sleepwalkers. The fact that it is men who sleepwalk, accentuates the anxiety about society's double-standards and the way they affect women.

The moonstone and the Shivering Sand are connected to the phases of the moon, which is symbolic of femininity. The moonstone and the Shivering sand are metaphors of femininity, which are concerned with the unknown: 'At the turn of the tide, something goes on in the unknown deeps below...' (p.237). The moonstone and the Shivering Sand bring about the chaos which Rachel and Rosanna endure throughout the narrative. Rosanna commits suicide as she can no longer contain her love for Blake

---

[7] A.S.Weber, *19th Century Science: A selection of original texts* (Canada: Broadview, 2000), p.200.

and Rachel isolates herself from everyone once the diamond has been taken. On the night of Rachel's birthday dinner, Blake sleepwalks into Rachel's room and takes the diamond from the Indian cabinet:

> 'Your eyes were bright-brighter than usual. You looked about the room, as if you knew you were where you ought to be...I saw the gleam of the stone between your finger and thumb, when you took your hand out'[8]

Blake's act of taking the diamond on the night of Rachel's eighteenth birthday party, implies his claim to her virginity, hence, it is his way of possessing her. Once Rachel recognizes that the diamond is missing, she cries 'my diamond is gone!' Evidently, the diamond is of sentimental value to Rachel, because it is an article that she can call her own. In order to understand the importance of the diamond to Rachel, it is worth stating the status of women at the time Collins was writing in. Married women of the middle and upper classes had been defined legally by the doctrine of coverture, as objects rather than subjects with rights. A husband was responsible for his wife's actions, and he controlled her property. Unmarried women of these classes were dependant on father/brother and then subsequently husband, who had access to their fortunes, which is why Godfrey Ablewhite is eager to form an alliance with Rachel, to claim her inheritance.

Jewellery is an important item to female characters, because they are objects that they can claim possession of. It is worth cross-referencing to Sigmund Freud's 'Analysis of a Case of Hysteria' (1905). Yet again, the possession of jewellery is presented to the reader in psychoanalytical terms as a way for Dora's mother to save herself. Dora recounts a recurring dream in which her father reprimands her mother for preferring to save her jewellery box rather than her children from a burning house:

> 'Mother is very fond of jewellery and had a lot given to her by father... mother wanted to be given particular pearl drops to wear in her ears. But father did not like that kind of thing, and he

---
[8] Wilkie Collins, *The Moonstone* (Oxford: Oxford University Press, 1982), p.386/387. All further references to this text are given parenthetically in the dissertation.

brought her a bracelet instead of the drops. She was furious and told him that as he had spent so much money on a present she did not like he had better give it to someone else[9]

To both Dora's mother and Rachel, jewellery is a personal asset, because it represents themselves. It is easy to sympathise with Rachel because the moonstone is her possession and is presented as an extension of her body and virginity: 'Rachel was showing the Indians the diamond in he bosom of her dress' (p.67). Once the moonstone is taken away from Rachel, another meaning is attributed to it. Blake takes the moonstone and Ablewhite takes it from him and wants to have the diamond cut into pieces. This suggests that Rachel's value is not in her wholeness and individuality but in her multiplicity as wife/mother/caregiver. Lucy Irigaray acknowledges this point by stating:

> Once [virgins] are divided, cut up, married, they become use value recognized only for their ability to reproduce themselves. Rachel and her (uncut) diamond are both valued in a capitalist economy for their potential than for themselves[10]

The status of women is presented negatively in the moonstone, because women are not subjects, they are objects in the eyes of society and are expected to fulfil their duties as Irigaray points out. In *The Moonstone*, there is an anxiety regarding female sexuality, which is why both Rachel and Rosanna are claimed. Rachel is a strong willed and outspoken young woman, Rosanna Spearman as her surname implies, does not have a favourable outlook of men. Rosanna identifies herself in turn with the sands that suffocate hundreds of people:

> All sinking lower and lower in the dreadful deeps! Throw a stone in, Mr. Betteredge! Throw a stone in and let's see the sand suck it down! (p.28)

---

[9] Sigmund Freud, 'Dora' and 'Little Hans', trans. Alix & James Strachey ed., James Strachey (London: Penguin, 1990), p. 134.
[10] Lucy Irigaray, *The Sex Which is Not One*, 1977, trans. Catherine Porter (Ithaca: NY, 1985), p.186.

There is something masochistic in the way that Rosanna takes pleasure in seeing the 'sand suck' the stones down. The Shivering Sand is a place of destruction in the way that objects are pulled down and the fact that Rosanna goes to this place, says something about her threatening sexuality. For instance, when Franklin probes the Sands with a stick to find a chest left by Rosanna, the combination of sexual excitement and sexual fear seems to permeate the diction that Collins uses:

> In this position, my face was within a few feet of the surface of the quicksand. The sight of it near me, still disturbed at intervals by its hideous shivering fit, shook my nerves for the moment. A horrible fancy that the dead woman might appear on the scene of her suicide, to assist my search - an unutterable dread of seeing her rise through the heavy surface of the sane, and point to the place - forced itself into my mind, and turned me cold in the warm sunlight. I own I closed my eyes at the moment when the point of the stick first entered the quicksand. The instant afterwards, before the stick entered the quicksand, before the stick could have been submerged more than a few inches. I was free from the hold of my own superstitious terror, and was throbbing with excitement from head to foot. (p.343)

The effect this long quotation has is that it merges the concept of untamed sexuality with destruction. Collins' language here is highly sensational in the way that the diction used is full of contrasts: 'horrible fancy', 'turned me cold in the warm sunlight' and 'superstitious terror… and throbbing with excitement from head to foot'. The effect these words have is that they mirror Blake's uncertainty and excitement about the unknown, which is sex, but more specifically, female sexuality. Furthermore, the concept of the unknown is stressed upon in this quotation as Rosanna has had to conceal information, which has led to her self–destruction. In other words, the anxiety here is somewhat to do with Rosanna's sexuality, but also about the silence which she and Rachel adopt.

On a broader perspective, it is not so much Rosanna's sexuality which causes 'terror', but male behaviour. If autonomy is firmly placed in male hands, so is guilt. Rachel and Rosanna are individually not collusively guilty, of shielding the man they both love. Though the women are innocent of crime, they are culpable in another way, as they do not divulge information about what took place the night the diamond was taken. Rachel realizes this and exclaims: 'they protect men, where they should expose them'. This is where Collins criticizes society's gender codes in the novel, by submitting to the expectations of society, then women such as Rosanna and Rachel will provide a safe haven for male egos. The message that Collins is filtering through is that women compound men's errors and crimes because they are expected to be passive creatures. Collins drew upon Nancy in Charles Dickens' *Oliver Twist* (1838) who protects Oliver, which leads to her fateful death. Collins looked upon Nancy as 'the finest thing he [Dickens] ever did. I never afterwards saw all sides of a woman's character'[11]. There appears to be a contradiction in Collins' perception of Nancy, Rachel and Rosanna. On the one hand he viewed Nancy as 'the finest thing', but in his novel, he does not condone Rachel and Rosanna's silence, instead it leads Rachel to behave hysterically and Rosanna to commit suicide. Contradiction plays an ongoing role in the novel between conscious/unconscious, morals/crime, silence/destruction, women/sexuality and Christian religion/secular religion. These contradictions are important when analysing Blake's sleepwalking incident, because it says something of the way society needs to change its outlook on male and female subject positions, as there are many sides of seeing an individual.

Rachel's characterization is a good example of how contradictions work against each other. Rachel's secrecy and self-control, would have been considered feminine virtues in the nineteenth century, however these traits are considered as 'odd' and 'wild' to Lady Verinder and Bruff, the lawyer. The irony of course is that if Rachel was outspoken, then she would confess her feelings for Blake like Rosanna, and then she might suffer the same fate as her. Instead, Rachel constrains her feelings for Blake and it is not until chapter seven of 'The Discovery of the Truth' that Rachel's hysterical behaviour is presented:

> 'I am worse, if worse can be, than you are yourself.' Sobs and tears burst from her. She struggled with them fiercely ... 'I can't tear you out of my heart... even now! You may trust in the shameful,

---

[11] *Pall Mall Gazette*, 50 (20.1.1890).

shameful weakness which can only struggle against you in this way! O God! I despise myself even more heartily than I despise him!' (p.393)

For most of this chapter she is represented as moving automatically and her actions are governed by her body not mind, in the way that she is described as 'acting under some influence independent of her will' (p.379). The fact that Rachel 'struggled' with her feelings, re-emphasizes the whole dilemma of the novel, which is the inability of characters to consciously transgress. If Rachel contravenes social ideals then she will be considered 'loose' or 'fallen' because society deems that she should be passive. Rosanna like Rachel is another victim of a character unable to subvert society's morals, because her past returns to hinder her position within the Verinder household. Rosanna was a 'thief before repenting' (p.23) and entering the Reformatory from which Lady Verinder hired her. Once the moonstone has been removed, Rosanna is the first suspect to be implicated by sergeant Cuff.

This is set side by side with characters such as Godfrey Ablewhite and Drusilla Clack. Godfrey is used as a device to critique the way that society is more concerned with appearance than people's conduct. When Godfrey is introduced into the narrative, one would expect him to be a good and honourable man, which his surname 'white' alludes to. However, as the novel progresses, organized Christian religion (which Ablewhite and Clack are representative of), is presented as hypocritical and mercenary. Ablewhite wants to marry Rachel, not because he loves her, but because he is in love with her inheritance. At the end of the novel, it is revealed that not only did Ablewhite take the diamond from the unconscious Blake, but he was leading a double life. Ablewhite is discovered by sergeant Cuff and Blake at The Wheel of Fortune; wearing make up and a fake beard. The effect this has is that appearances are not what they seem; English society suspects Indian intruders to be responsible for crimes on English soil when in fact it was John Herncastle, an English man who committed this crime. With such contradictions, it is not surprising that the ending is ambiguous. The text ends with the marriage between Rachel and Blake; however Bettredge's words cloud this happy ending:

So the years pass, and repeat each other; so the same events revolve in the cycles of time. What will be the next adventures of the moonstone? Who can tell'? (p. 522)

Bettredge's words do not give closure to the ending. Instead the tone is ominous in the way that the moonstone might have been removed from the Verinder household, but it still exists and could cause disarray if it was ever taken away from the Hindu temple. Having said that, Bettredge's reference to the moonstone as an 'adventure' is hyperbolic, considering it has been the cause of disorder than adventure in the Verinder household.

In Collins' *The Law and the Lady* and George Eliot's *The Mill on the Floss*, physical sleepwalking does not take place. Instead, there is a reference to Vincenzo Bellini's opera *La Sonnambula* (the sleepwalker). The opera depicts Amina, an orphan girl who on the eve of being married to a young farmer, sleepwalks into Count Roda'lfo's chambers. Amina, unaware of what has passed, is accused by Elvino, her fiancée of partaking in an illicit relationship with the count; thus, their relationship comes to an end. It is not until the end of the opera, that Elvino sees the sleepwalking Amina issuing herself from a window in the roof and descending to the ground by a ruinous flight of steps. Amina's sleepwalking can be attributed to her anxiety about married life and assuming a new social position as wife and subsequently mother.

The inclusion of *La Sonnambula* in Collins' and Eliot's novel represents the unknown to Valeria and Maggie. More so, it is a foreshadowing of the new positions that both women will assume. It is perhaps worth taking a moment to examine the role of women in opera and how it relates to Valeria and Maggie. In the eighteenth century, women in opera had little voice because their roles were passive and submissive. Women were part of what Catherine Clément calls a 'social pyramid', which was constructed of the monarch/husband at the top, which was followed by women. However, by the time Bellini wrote *La Sonnambula* (1831), the female role had undergone considerable change. Instead of the obedient wife/mother/daughter, women in nineteenth century opera, 'end up punished-fallen, abandoned, or dead'[12]. This information is important when reading *The*

---

[12] Catherine Clément, *Opera, or the Undoing of Women*, trans. Betsy Wing (Minnesota: The University of Minnesota, 1988), p.7.

Law and the Lady and *The Mill on the Floss* because the reference to *La Sonnambula* suggests that Valeria and Maggie are in danger of risking their reputations. This is somewhat true in both texts as Valeria refuses to pursue Eustace's case as she might be abandoned by him. Maggie's moral and sexual transgression leads her to be punished in the form of death for her elopement with Stephen Guest.

In Collins' text, the reference to the opera is made in chapter nine 'The Major's Defeat', where Valeria is searching for clues about Eustace's past in Major Fitz-David's house. Valeria states: 'At the moment when I first heard her, she was singing the lovely air from the *Sonnambula*' (p.73). This chapter is a pivotal chapter in the sense that it is a prelude to Valeria's discovery of her husband's former marriage and the trial concerning the death of Sara Macallan. Thus, Collins' insertion of *La Sonnambula* in this chapter is used as a device to present the uncertainty of Valeria's identity and the law. It is in the subsequent chapter that Valeria discovers the truth about Eustace and his identity:

> A first glance showed me that it represented the portraits of two persons.
> One of the persons I recognized as my husband.
> The other person was a woman.
> Her face was entirely unknown to me...
> At the back of the portraits, the lines ran this:-
> 'To Major Fitz-David, with two vases. From his friends S. and E.M.'...
> 'S. and E.M.'? Those last two letters might stand for the initials of my husband's name-his true name- Eustace Macallan[13]

In chapter eleven 'The Return to Life', Valeria is given insight into Eustace's trials:

> 'Eustace was tried in Scotland' he said. 'There is a verdict allowed by Scottish law, which (so far as I know) is not permitted by the laws of any other civilized country on the face of earth. When

---

[13] Wilkie Collins, *The Law and the Lady* (Oxford: Oxford University Press, 1992), p.88/89. All further references to this text are given parenthetically in the dissertation.

the jury are in doubt whether to condemn or acquit the prisoner brought before them, they are permitted, in Scotland, to express that doubt by a form of compromise... they extricate themselves from the difficulty by finding a verdict of Not Proven.' (p.101)

These two quotations show just how much is unknown to Valeria. These examples illustrate how identity is easy to assume and discarded, because if Valeria had not discovered all this information, then she would be living in a state of oblivion. It is interesting that the major speaks disdainfully of the Scottish criminal system, pointing out that the verdict of Not Proven is 'not permitted by the laws of any other civilized country' (p.101).

In Collins' address to the reader, he says 'to remember (first): that the actions of human beings are not invariably governed by the laws of pure reason'. The question that Collins fails to provide an answer for is 'what is reason'? From what has been established about the Scottish legal system, where is the logic of having a jury who are in 'doubt whether to condemn or acquit the prisoner brought before them'? It is not only Valeria's identity which is called into question, but also Eustace's identity as an innocent or guilty man. From the very beginning of the novel, there is uneasiness about this issue of identity. For example, Valeria signs the marriage register incorrectly by using her married, not maiden name:

> In the confusion of the moment... I committed a mistake ominous, I signed my married instead of my maiden name. (p.8)

When Eustace signs the register, Valeria notices that 'his hands trembled too, and he produced a very poor specimen of his customary signature'. Clearly, there is something distressing about this wedding. Instead of the marriage being a day of celebration, it is presented as a day of restlessness and bad luck; in the way that Aunt Starkweather states 'A bad beginning... I hope you may not live to regret it'. Moreover, Valeria's wedding dress is described as 'studiously concealing, instead of proclaiming that she had been married that morning' (p.11).

From these examples, the wedding itself has no identity of its own, it is described in mundane terms, in the way that the atmosphere is described as 'heavy and damp', 'dreary' and 'dull' (p.9). The effect these words have is that they are a foreboding of the separation between Eustace and Valeria and the truth about Eustace's former marriage and murder trial. In addition, it is interesting that chapter one opens with an excerpt from the marriage service of the Church of England:

> 'For this manner in the old time the holy women also, who trusted in God, adorned themselves, being in subjection unto their own husbands' (p.8)

The irony of these words is that if Valeria were to be subordinate to Eustace, then she would be living a life with a phoney identity. Furthermore, criminal law is presented as a set of rigid rules, which does not help people:

> 'My defence was undertaken by the greatest lawyers in the land,' he said. 'After such men have done their utmost, and have failed-my poor Valeria, what can you, what can I, do? We can only submit'. (p. 107)

The law is presented as something sinister in the way that Eustace says 'We can only submit'. What makes Eustace's actions distressing is that the law does not protect Valeria from marrying Eustace who adopts an alias name. At the same time, the law does not fully acquit Eustace from a crime which he never committed. Valeria's response that 'the law has failed to do for you, your wife must do for you' (p.116), polarizes the law on one end and human behaviour on the other.

Valeria's response and actions defy social law as she crosses beyond the domestic arena. By rejecting social convention, Valeria is asserting her real identity as an intelligent and head strong woman. For instance, Valeria travels to Spain upon receiving a telegram stating that 'Mr. Eustace is severely wounded in a skirmish, by a stray shot'. (p.306). Her response is that of a determined and confident woman:

> I am going to the Foreign Office about my passport- I have some interest there: they can give me letters; they can advice and assist me. I leave to-night by the mail train to Calais!

Valeria travels to Edinburgh in search of any evidence in Gleninch: 'I shall continue to join the lawyer in Edinburgh after meeting my husband in London' (p.365). Valeria travels to Paris upon request from Eustace and Mrs Macallan: 'he is helpless in his bed... he asks you to join him in Paris' (p.367). These examples show how Valeria defines her own identity as a woman, not society, as she is capable of being an independent woman, which social law denies her.

The theme of fixed gender identities is an important aspect of the novel in relation to the instability of the individual. Dexter is a key character in this text, as he has the ability to play with identity and undermine the concept of defined gender. Through the characterization, the effect of having Dexter in this novel is that he questions the way masculinity is constructed:

> His face was bright with vivacity and intelligence. His large, clear blue eyes, and his long, delicate white hands, were like the eyes and hands of a beautiful woman. He would have looked effeminate, but for the manly proportions of his throat and chest: aided in their effect by his flowing beard and long moustache. (p. 173)

Dexter embodies a *mélange* of masculine and feminine traits, which makes him a complicated character to pin down, because he is biologically a man, but possesses 'eyes and hands of a beautiful woman'. Dexter plays a crucial role in the novel, as he has knowledge of the truth behind Sara's death but refuses to reveal it. Instead, the truth has to emerge through the disintegration of consciousness and the piecing together of the fragments of his memory:

> 'What did the Missus say to the Maid?'...He went on speaking, more and more vacantly, more and more rapidly. 'The mistress said to the Maid, "We've got him off. What about the letter? Burn it now. No fire in the grate. No matches in the box. House topsy turvey. Servants all gone. Tear it up. Waste paper. Throw it away. Gone for ever. Oh, Sara, Sara, Sara. Gone for ever. (p.345)

Dexter is a character in which oppositions come together to form an individual, as consciousness and madness merge together to present the truth of how Sara was killed. Jenny Bourne Taylor acknowledges this representation of Dexter:

> Dexter spears as the unexpected juxtaposing of fragments that can be recognized but not reconciled: "a strange and startling creature- literally the half of a man... Never had nature committed a more careless or a more cruel mistake than in the making of this man, "My chair is me" pushes physiological psychology to an absurd conclusion[14]

It is not only the representation of Dexter that is 'not reconciled', but the representation of masculinity.

Eustace does not appear to be masculine in the way that he is presented. Eustace escapes to Spain and is injured and weak:

> He has joined a charitable brotherhood; and he is off to the war in Spain with a red cross on his arm, when he ought to be here on his knees asking his wife to forgive him. I say that is the conduct of a weak man. Some people might call it by a harder name. (p. 196)

What makes Eustace' actions confusing are that he would go to Spain and fight, but does not fight to prove his innocence or to save his marriage. It is interesting how at the beginning of the novel, Eustace's hands are said to have 'trembled' to produce 'a very poor specimen of his customary signature'. Later on in the novel, he sends a letter to Valeria from Paris whereby his handwriting is described as 'containing two lines traced in pencil, traced in pencil- oh, so feebly and wearily!' (p.367). The effect these two examples have is that they show how Eustace fails to assert his identity in the form of writing. Diction such as 'trembled', 'feebly' and 'wearily', re-emphasize Eustace's inability to express himself as an individual, which probably explains why he is absent throughout the duration of the novel.

---

[14] Jenny Bourne Taylor, *In the Secret Theatre of Home: Wilkie Collins, Sensation narrative and nineteenth-century psychology* (London: Routledge, 1988), p.46/47

It is ironic how Mrs Macallan tells Valeria once she takes charge of the investigation that 'I cannot let you uselessly risk your reputation and your happiness' (p.198). No one questions Eustace or his actions, as he decides to leave his wife because she wants to secure his reputation as an innocent man. Furthermore, Valeria is expected to give up her enquiry into the investigation, because Eustace will not return to her if she continues to do so:

> "Has she given up that idea? Can you positively say she has given up that idea?" Over and over again, he has put those questions to me. I have answered - what else could I do, in the miserable feeble state in which he still lies? - I have answered in such a manner as to soothe and satisfy him. I have said, "Relieve your mind of all anxiety on that subject: Valeria has no choice but to give up the idea"... In the other event- that is to say, if you are still determined to preserve in your hopeless project-then make up your mind to face the result. Set Eustace's prejudices at defiance in this particular; and you lose your hold on his gratitude, his penitence, and his love-you will in my belief, never see him again. (p.361)

Eustace's attitude demonstrates how women such as Valeria are expected to make allowances for men, but when it comes to Eustace he is exempt from having his irresponsibility questioned. The point is why should Valeria have to choose between the investigation and her marriage, when she is more than capable of doing both? Instead, Valeria chooses to withdraw from the investigation, otherwise she will not have a reputation or a husband:

> That morning, I wrote again to Mr Playmore; telling him what my position was, and withdrawing, definitively, from all share in investigation the mystery which lay hidden under the dust-heap at Gleninch. (p.368)

If Valeria wants to safeguard her reputation then all she can do is return to the role that society has assigned to her, and that is the submissive wife. Valeria, Eustace and Dexter have been used in this discussion to question women's social positions and the representation of masculinity. At the end of the novel, Collins places Valeria as an active wife and mother, Eustace is the head of the household and Dexter dies:

> He closed his eyes in slumber, and never woke again. So for this man too the end came mercifully, without grief or pain! (p.407)

Thus, the ending restores order, but what negates this order is the fact that it has been the actions of human behaviour that has triumphed over the law. Valeria like Priscilla in "Who Killed Zebedee?" exercises what she feels is justice, and obtains it without having to use the law. The reference to *La Sonnambula* is important because from what has been said, the past and unknown has been explored, and it is through the discovery of the unknown that Valeria and Eustace achieve ipseity.

In *The Mill on the Floss*, the reference to *La Sonnambula* is in Book six chapter seven, when Philip sings the tune from the opera:

> 'Don't you know that?' - said Philip, bringing out the tune more definitely. 'It's from the Sonnambula ... it appears the tenor is telling the heroine that he shall always love her though she may forsake him'[15]

Philip's words that the heroine 'may forsake' the tenor, is a foreboding of Maggie's eventual elopement with Stephen Guest. This is one of the most important chapters because it prognosticates what will happen in the novel. The fact that this chapter is placed in a volume entitled 'The Great Temptation' emphasizes Maggie's growing feelings for Stephen, but also her 'fall'. Maggie is overwhelmed by emotion, to the extent that it controls her, in the same way that Angel Clare is controlled by emotion.

The references made to water in this chapter symbolize the way in which Maggie is being drowned by emotion, which forebodes her literal drowning at the end of the novel. Chapter seven is full of water imagery: 'The next morning was very wet' (p.524), 'we are all a little damped by the rain' (p.531) and Maggie is said to be 'borne along by a wave too strong for

---

[15] George Eliot, *The Mill on the Floss* (London: Penguin, 1985), p.533. All further references to this text are given parenthetically in the essay.

her' (p.534). Water imagery is connected with Maggie and femininity, from destroying her curls with water as a child, her destiny is likened to the river:

> Maggie's destiny, then, is at present hidden, and we must wait for it to reveal itself like the course of an unmapped river. (pp.514-515)

The river is symbolic of the current of sexual desire and passion, the force of Maggie's temptation, the suspension of her awareness and moral conscience and the eventual consequences of this sexual desire. For example on the streamer, water imagery conveys her feelings of freedom from her ties and responsibilities, and from the struggle between her desire and conscience:

> But now nothing was distinct to her: she was being lulled to sleep with that soft stream still flowing over her, with those delicious visions melting and fading like the wondrous aerial land of the west. (p.595)

Chapter seven is a pivotal section; in the same way that chapter nine is important in *The Law and the Lady*. In this chapter, Maggie interacts with Philip and Stephen, two very different men. When Philip enters the Deane household, Maggie's dilemma is presented very clearly to the reader:

> They were not painful tears: they had rather something of the same origin as the tears women and children shed when they have found some protection to cling to, and look back on the threatened danger. (p.525)

Maggie's feelings for Stephen are a 'danger' to her, because they contravene social morals. But what this quotation presents is the dilemma which Maggie faces between protection and danger. On the one hand, Maggie feels protected in the presence of Philip, but as this chapter reveals, there is a 'cold indifference' between the pair. Thus, Philip is not compatible with the passionate Maggie. However, Stephen is not a good suitor for Maggie because he is a danger, as he incites sexual desire and passion, rather than feelings of pure love. The inclusion of the *Sonnambula* simply re-emphasizes Maggie's unawareness of her position, and her failure to recognize that neither Philip nor Stephen are good lovers for her. Instead, this chapter is a foreboding of Maggie's *ad lib* sexual feelings, which leads to her tragic fate. For instance, when Maggie begins to ponder about Stephen, the way that she is described highlights her predicament:

> It was a thought that made her shudder: it gave new definiteness to her present position, and to the tendency of what had happened the evening before. She moved her arm from the table, urged to change her position by that positive physical oppression at the heart that sometimes a sudden mental pang. (p.529)

Diction such as 'shudder' and 'mental pang' denotes the effect that Stephen has on Maggie. There is something unsettling in the way that Maggie is presented, because the way she is described is contradictory. For example she has a 'new definiteness to her present position', this is countered by her thought that she should 'change her position by that positive physical oppression'. This description depicts the state of disorder which looms in Maggie's mind, because she is torn between reason and desire. Furthermore, the alliteration of the 'p' sound in 'positive' and 'physical' re-emphasizes the intensity of Maggie's mental anarchy. Maggie's oppression is linked into a later comment made by the narrator that she is 'borne along a wave too strong for her'. These two quotations are a reflection of Maggie's repression by society and her family. Furthermore, these quotations are a foreboding of her being drowned at the end of the novel: 'The boat reappeared - but brother and sister had gone down in an embrace never to be parted' (p.655). The point here is that Maggie is a victim of oppression regardless if she follows society or her own feelings, either way she is doomed to live a tragic life.

Chapter seven brings out all these key ideas in the way that Maggie views Philip and Stephen. For example, when Stephen is singing, she is said to be 'quivering' and 'clasping' as 'her eyes dilated and brightened' (p.532). In contrast, Maggie is 'touched not thrilled' by Philip's song (p.533), but Stephen's 'saucy energy' has a great effect on her:

> In spite of her resistance to the spirit of the song and to the singer, [Maggie] was taken hold of and shaken by the influence. (p. 534)

The tone in which the narrator relates Maggie's feelings is pessimistic in the way that she is 'taken hold of and shaken'. Maggie is like a sleepwalker in that she is controlled by her emotions than being in control of them. Ergo, the reference to the *Sonnambula* merely re-emphasizes this whole idea of the unknown to both Valeria and Maggie, if they choose to follow their instincts and defy social convention. In both cases, Valeria and Maggie are reverted back to their positions as submissive / repressed women. Valeria rejects the investigation and is reinstated back into the home: 'The place is my bedroom' (p.410) and Maggie is silenced through death, when she is drowned.

The theme of law and justice dominates Wilkie Collins' novella "Who Killed Zebedee?" As the title suggests, the story is pre-occupied with the search for the person who killed Zebedee. Furthermore, the title goes as far as to imply that there is chaos, because the story is pre-occupied with the search for the murderer. It is not so much the murder which causes confusion, but sleepwalking. The significance of sleepwalking in this story is that it allows murder to take place. In other words, murder is disguised under the masquerade of sleepwalking, which allows the murderer to escape justice for his/her crime. This text questions the role of the law and the police and at the same time depicts the police's negligence in pursuing their investigation to find the real murderer. Collins deliberately implicates Mrs Zebedee as the prime suspect because it she who exclaims: 'My dear John's murdered! I am the miserable wretch- I did it in my sleep!' (p.9). Additionally, it would be hard not to suspect Mrs Zebedee as the accomplice as she has a history of sleepwalking:

> The one objection to her had been the occasional infirmity of sleepwalking, which made it necessary that one of the other female servants should sleep in the same room, with the door locked and the key under the pillow[16]

With this in mind, on the night of the murder, Mrs Zebedee tells the speaker that she was reading a book entitled *The World of Sleep*, which would have most likely induced an unconscious reaction to kill her husband, after reading one of the cases:

---

[16] Wilkie Collins, "Who Killed Zebedee?" (London: Hesperus Press Limited, 2002), p.14. All further references to this text are given parenthetically in the essay.

> There was one terrible story which took a hold on my mind- the story of a man who stabbed his own wife in a sleepwalking dream. I thought of putting down my book after that, and then changed my mind again and went on... I don't know what o'clock it was when I went to sleep. There was a spare candle on the chimney-piece. I found the matchbox, and got a light. Then, for the first time, I turned round towards the bed; and had seen the dead body of her husband, murdered while she was unconsciously at his side. (p.16)

Mrs Zebedee's words are important because boundaries of innocence and guilt are put into question early on in the text. If Mrs Zebedee did commit the crime, is she innocent because she was unconscious? Or is she guilty for committing the crime, irrespective of her state of mind?

When the enquiry into the investigation is resumed and Mrs Zebedee is put into the witness box, she divulges more evidence which neither secures her innocence or guilt as a suspect:

> Only three questions of importance were put to her. First, the knife was produced. Had she ever seen it in her husband's possession? Never. Did she know anything about it? Nothing whatever. Secondly, did she, or did her husband, lock the bedroom door when they returned from the theatre? No. Did she afterwards lock the door herself? No. Thirdly, had she any sort of reason to give for supposing that she had murdered her husband in a sleepwalking dream? No reason, except that she was beside herself at the time, and the book put the thought into her head. (pp.17-18).

From the above quotation, it is easy to see how the conscious and unconscious fuse together to create confusion. On the one hand, Mrs Zebedee could be innocent because she has no knowledge of the murder weapon, and the bedroom door was not locked, which would allow another person to have access to their bedroom and commit the crime. However, with a record of sleepwalking, Mrs Zebedee would not have any recollection that she had murdered her husband because she would have been unconscious. The fact that the 'book put the thought into head', would make her more than capable of committing the act. This citation is highly perplexing in that this case questions how the law defines who is innocent or guilty. Sleepwalking poses another dilemma for the law. In this story, sleepwalking has been used as an excuse to commit a crime by someone other than the sleepwalker, i.e. Priscilla. The point here is that if other crimes are taking place through the disguise of sleepwalking or other mental distresses such as hysteria, then it is not surprising that criminals cannot be caught and sentenced.

Throughout this story, parallels such as the conscious/unconscious and innocent /guilty are presented to the reader. One such parallel is criminal justice and individual justice, which has been analysed in *The Law and the Lady*. In the story there is an inspector and the police who are representative of the state's law, but there is Priscilla and the speaker, who implement what they consider to be their own sense of justice. Priscilla for instance, is like Tess in Hardy's novel, in the way that social law has failed her. The speaker discovers that Zebedee was a 'vicious and heartless wretch' to Priscilla in their former relationship:

> They were engaged- and, I add with indignation, he tried to seduce her under a promise of marriage... The banns were published in my church. On the next day Zebedee disappeared, and cruelly deserted her. (p.28)

One cannot help but feel sympathy for Priscilla and the way she was treated or mistreated by Zebedee. This is not to say that Zebede's murder is condoned, but it cannot be condemned because society has allowed him to behave in a dishonourable way. One can go as far as to pose the question: if Priscilla had deserted Zebedee, would she be able to escape responsibility for her actions?

The same moral which is presented in Tess, is stressed upon in Collins' story. The moral is that social law does not protect women, but endangers them. The speaker is told that Zebedee tried to 'seduce her under the promise of marriage', which demonstrates how men like Zebedee and Alec can take advantage of their positions as men, to achieve what they want. At no point in the Rector's letter to the speaker, does he mention anything about Zebedee's actions being reproached by society. Instead, it is Priscilla's murder of Zebedee which causes an outcry and makes the speaker bewildered:

> I stepped forward - and she saw my face. My face silenced her. I spoke in the fewest words I could find...
> 'There is the unfinished inscription on the knife, completed in your handwriting. I could hang you by a word...' (pp.28-29)

It is interesting that Priscilla is 'silenced' by the speaker's face. This could be attributed to the fact that she suspects the speaker has knowledge of her past and involvement in the murder. It can also reiterate the idea of Priscilla having to be silenced by another man, which is something she had to do after Zebedee's desertion. If this is the case then it highlights an important dilemma which Priscilla and Tess face. From reading this text and *Tess of the d'Urbervilles*, there are only two options available to women: they can either remain silent about being raped or deserted by a former lover, or they can avenge the men who have maltreated them, and pay the penalty. Basically, social law in these two texts is defined as a law which questions women, but not men for transgressing moral law. Ergo, if social law does not protect and give justice to women, then to someone like Priscilla who has been ill-treated, she will execute her own definition of justice:

> The devil entered into me when I tried their door, on my way up to bed, and found it unlocked... I had the knife in my hand, and the thought came to me to do it, so that they might hang her for murder. I couldn't take the knife out again, when I had done it. (pp.29-30)

Once the inspector suspends the murder investigation, the speaker decides to take the law into hands and decides to pursue it:

> The assassination of the poor young husband soon passed out of notice, like other undiscovered murders. One obscure person only was foolish enough... to persist in trying to solve the problem of who killed Zebedee... he held to his own ambition though everybody laughed at him. In plain English, I was the man. (p.20)

The speaker seems to be isolated in the way that he describes himself as 'obscure' and 'held to his own ambition'; which is in contrast to everybody mocking him for following his instincts. Collins intentionally makes his character delve further into the investigation, because it points out the flaws in the inspector's research:

> We had none of us remembered that a certain portion of cutlers might be placed, by circumstances, out of our reach-either by retiring from business or becoming bankrupt. (p.24)

It is the inspector who is 'laughed at' not the speaker, for not anticipating the personal/financial status of the cutlers. Due to the police's half-hearted investigation, the speaker comes across Mr Scorrier, a cutler who is not aware that Zebedee was murdered, but it was the same cutler that Priscilla has the knife engraved:

> 'The knife was bought of my late brother-in-law, in the shop downstairs... A person in a state of frenzy burst into this very room, and snatched the knife away from me, when I was only halfway through the inscription!' I read the complete inscription, intended for the knife that killed Zebedee, and written as follows: 'To John Zebedee. From Priscilla Thurlby'. (pp.25-26)

The conscious and unconscious work together here to discover who the murderer is. If Mr. Scorrier read newspapers, then he would have told the police who the knife belonged to. Furthermore, if it was not for the speaker's initiative, then the murderer would not be discovered; which contrasts to the police's inability to see past appearances and conduct professional examination of the case. It is interesting that the speaker says in his penitence: 'Many people think I deserve to be hanged myself for not having given her up to the gallows' (p.30). The speaker's words bring to a close the theme of what justice means to the individual and society. If other people think that Priscilla should be hanged for her crime, then surely Zebedee should also be questioned for his behaviour. This is not to argue that Zebedee should be hanged, but if society has one law then it should be applied to all, irrespective of gender or ethnicity. One can argue that if society protected women, then Priscilla would not use sleepwalking as a guise to murder Zebedee.

This idea of sleepwalking providing a way of expressing duality or contradictions appears in Hardy's *Tess of the d'Urbervilles*. Purity and sexuality complicate the way that Tess is presented to Angel, Alec and the reader. Sleepwalking takes place in chapter thirty-seven of the novel. Angel Clare, sleepwalking, takes Tess out of her room and lays her in an abbot's stone coffin. The narrator's depiction of Angel's sleepwalking seems to suggest that Angel has no sense of agency, but is controlled by some 'other' external force:

> Under the influence of any strongly disturbing force Clare would occasionally walk in his sleep, and even perform strange feats, such as he had done on the night of their return from the market just before their marriage, when he re-enacted in his bedroom his combat wit the man who had insulted her. Tess saw that continued metal distress had wrought him into that somnambulistic state… murmuring he said "My poor Tess, my dearest darling Tess! So sweet, so good, so true!"[17]

Angel is said to be 'under the influence' of 'any strongly disturbing force' whilst he is sleepwalking, which suggests that Angel is controlled by his repressed emotions, in relation to Tess's innocence. Angel's 'combat with the man who had insulted her' is an extension of Angel's complex and suppressed mind. Angel's 'hidden place' is the conflict between the way society and he should reject Tess on the one hand and his love for her, on the other: 'Angel took advantage of the support of the handrail to imprint a kiss upon her lips – lips in the daytime scorned'. Sleepwalking is important in this chapter as the reader gains access to Angel's unconscious behaviour. This implies that Angel knows deep down that Tess in not in any way to blame for Alec's indecent assault on her, which is emphasized by his words 'Poor poor Tess, my dearest darling Tess… so sweet, so good, so true'. Angel's words allow the reader insight into his real feelings for her.

---

[17] Thomas Hardy, *Tess of the d'Urbervilles* (Oxford: Oxford University Press, 1983), p.242. All further references to this text are given parenthetically in the dissertation.

He does not loathe her, but loves her in this sleepwalking scene, as Tess is a fallen woman in the eyes of society.

The fact that Hardy puts Angel in a sleepwalking state is significant, because he could have easily made Angel dream of entering Tess' room and picking her up and bestowing his affection upon her. The effect this sleepwalking scene is that it brings Angel's state of 'otherness' to life and presents a conflict between the exterior 'acceptable' self and a repressed self full of desire. The sleepwalking scene is a sensational chapter, which does not suggest a happy ending, in the way that pity and sadness are evoked: 'He might drown her if he would, it would be better than parting tomorrow to lead severed lives'. The pathos of Tess being placed in the abbot's tomb is important, as it prefigures her and Angel's arrival at Stonehenge in chapter fifty-seven and is a foreboding of her fateful execution in the subsequent chapter.

In the preceding chapter (fifty-eight), Tess returns home and is reproached by her mother for confessing her encounter with Alec to Angel: 'O you little fool-you little fool!' (p.328). When Tess overhears her father doubting the validity between Angel and herself, she decides to leave again. Tess's second return home mirrors her homecoming in chapter twelve. In chapter twelve, Tess returned home because Alec in the former chapter sexually abused her. In this chapter (thirty-eight), Tess returns because she is rejected by Angel. The effect this has is that it creates a symmetrical structure in the novel, which suggests that the individual is controlled in the same way a somnambulist is controlled. The effect this has is that it shows that the individual has no individuality in this society. Angel is controlled by a 'disturbing force', which leads him to sleepwalk and Tess is controlled by society and the way that it perceives her.

Tess is a figure that is controlled by the way society; Angel, Alec and the narrator see her. A good example of this is in chapter thirty-four when Tess and Angel are speaking of their past. Angel tells Tess of his encounter with a prostitute:

> ...he plunged into eight-and-forty hours' dissipation with a stranger. "Happily I awoke almost immediately to a sense of my folly," he continued. "I would have no more to say to her, and I came home". (p.189)

Words such as 'he plunged' and 'dissipation' highlight the sexual nature of Angel's liaison with the *fille de joie*. Tess' confession denies her any sense of individuality in the way that her confession is mediated through a description of the room along with the objects in it. Tess's words do not appear in direct quotation, she is a "stranger", like Angel's former lover who has no voice:

> She entered on her story of her acquaintance with Alec d'Urberville and its results, murmuring the words without flinching, and with her eyelids drooping down. (p.293)

Lloyd Davis agrees with the way that Tess has no authority over her words or actions, instead they are presented through the eyes of Angel or narrator:

> The structure of the text subdivides this description that substitutes for Tess's confession; so that the temporal slot of her narrative falls precisely into the blank space between the two divisions of the novel, 'phase the fourth' and 'phase the fifth'. This structural gap connects Tess's confession with the narrative instance of her rape, also a blank passage on the page falling between book phases'[18]

The fact that there are 'structural gaps' in the rape and confession scene, shows how Tess is controlled by Alec who abuses her body, Angel who rejects her and the narrator who does not give her license to be presented fully. One can go as far as to argue that it is Tess's body not her mind which is the focus in the novel. For example both Alec and Alex are struck by her beauty and desire her, and the narrator too, is concerned with her body rather than her confession:

> Their hands were still joined... Imagination might have beheld a Last Day luridness in this red-coaled glow, which fell on his face and hand, and on hers, peering into the loose hair about her brow, and firing the delicate skin underneath. A large shadow of her

---

[18] *Virginal Sexuality and Texuality in Victorian Literature*, ed., Lloyd Davis (New York: State University of New York Press, 1993), p.171.

> shape rose upon the wall and ceiling. She bent forward at which each diamond on her neck gave a sinister wink like a toad's... she entered on her story of her acquaintance of Alec d'Urberville and its results, murmuring the words. (p.190)

Tess's elided confession both erases Angel's version of her, while it also introduces a sexualized female body absent from its pure/angelic form. Diction such as 'red –coaled glow', 'firing', 'sinister' and 'large shadow', equates Tess with the devil or monster which shows that she is fallen in the eyes of Angel. Furthermore, it is interesting how the narrator refers to Tess' words as 'murmuring'. It is ironic that the narrator would say such a thing, considering that he describes in great length Tess's physique and yet fails to relate her words to the reader. The effect this has is that it shows how Tess's words are futile in the sense that irrespective if she was raped or not, she is ultimately responsible for the moral rectitude of any sexual conduct. The point that Hardy is stressing here is that Tess is 'responsible' in body because she is not mentally responsible hence, the title 'The Woman Pays'. In other words, women's positions within society are mechanical like Angel's sleepwalking episode; they have no voice or mind of their own, but are expected to submit to society's rules.

The narrator's detachment from the narrative is reiterated in chapter fifty-eight, in the way that the reader knows nothing of Angel and 'Liza-Lu's feelings, as they do not speak, but remain 'absolutely motionless' and move 'mechanically'. What symbolizes Tess is not her beauty, but a 'black flag'. In the same way that her voice is insufficient in the confession; so is her body at the end of the novel, it is as if she never lived. The point here is that individuality does not exist in Tess's society. One only has to look at chapter thirty, where Hardy is preoccupied with the evolution of science, in which the strangeness of 'modern life; is suggested in the metaphor of a feeler stretching out across the countryside. Tess is captured and put on display by the light of the steam engine as if she were a scientific object:

> The light of the engine flashed for a second upon Tess Durbeyfield's figure, motionless under the great holly tree...with the round bare arms, the rainy face and hair, the suspended attitude of a friendly

leopard at pause, the print gown of no date or fashion, and the cotton bonnet drooping on her brow. (p.251)

The effect, like the confession scene and ending of the novel, emphasizes the insignificance of the individual. The modern world does not accept Tess as a personality; she is simply a 'native existence' it finds 'uncongenial'. Tess is used by Hardy to represent the insoluble social and background follies of his day. She is a figure in which polarized oppositions like 'virgin' and 'whore' are deconstructed. Tess consistently embodies many contradictions. For example, she is a peasant who is an educated female; she speaks not only the dialect of her home but an educated Sixth Standard English; she is pure yet seen as an object of erotic desire as a victim she is also a murderess. Tess persona poses a problem for less multifaceted characters such as Angel and Alec who fail to understand her and perceive her wrongly. The complexity of Tess is depicted in the way that she has two representations: an erotic body and a cultural body. Her erotic body, concentrated in her mouth, entices male lust; her cultural body, constructed by moral values, generates rejection. J.B. Bullen expresses the inconsistency in Tess' representation:

> Tess's erotic body, the creation of 'nature', is warm and vibrant; her social body, violated by Alec, is construed by society as degenerate and impure. The desire which Tess's erotic body stimulates in Angel is extinguished by his knowledge of her cultural body. He was, says Hardy, 'a slave to custom and convention' and he is deceived by the cultural construction of Tess as 'fallen'. After the wedding he says to Tess that he felt that he had married a 'woman in [her] shape'. The two representations of Tess's body are incongruent, and it is this social misfitting that leads her to the gallows. (p.262)

In these examples Hardy is promulgating to the reader what is tacitly presented in Angel's sleepwalking scene which is, identity belongs to society not the individual. Tess is a victim of society's double standards, which seeks to punish innocent women, but fails to apply the same 'justice' to men.

One only has to read the ending of the text to fully acknowledge the double standards which exist in Tess's society. 'Liza-Lu the 'spiritualised image of Tess' (p.419), walks hand in hand with Angel Clare, which suggests a happy ending. Having said that, the relationship between the two characters contravenes moral law; since a man's marriage with his sister-in-law remained not only illegal, but also tainted with the stigma of incest until the passing of the 'Deceased Wife's Sister Act' in 1907. In light of what has been said, the ending is anything but a happy one. There is a contradiction in the way that both 'Liza-Lu and Angel stand before Tess's execution, an unjust execution because Tess is punished for her crime, whereas 'Liza-Lu and Angel's relationship violates social order, and yet they walk away. Hardy seems to suggest that society's morals should be upheld by both men and women, and that the law should protect women such as Tess.

'Who is he, this Invisible being that rules me?' Sleepwalking / The Gothic/ The Supernatural

Hysteria has an ancient and notorious history; it was first diagnosed in ancient Greece. The term hysteria is a word whose root origins (hystero) entered the English language from the Greek word for womb. Since Hippocrates' day, women were believed to suffer from 'womb furie' or 'uterine displacement'. The medical texts explained that the standard treatment was the manipulation of the genitals to orgasm, resulting in fluid discharge from the vagina. Noted author James Cowles Prichard defined somnambulism as:

> The most severe affection... most frequently connected with other disorders of the brain. In females it is often conjoined with hysteria[19]

Hysteria, caused by 'uterus neglect' was considered to manifest itself in delusional activity, such as sleepwalking. Female sexuality was such a concern in the Victorian era, that in 1869 George Taylor, invented a fantastic steam-powered vibrator called 'The Manipulator', which became the first electric vibrator to surface in the late nineteenth century. The vibrator became widely available to the medical profession and was considered a popular cure for all types of female related maladies.

---

[19] James Cowles Prichard, *Somnambulism and Animal Magnetism* (London, 1834), p.18.

In the Victorian epoch, there was an ongoing apprehension about female sexuality. The Victorians lived in a time of double standards, whereby men were not questioned for their behaviour, but women were sexually sanctioned. The root of women sleepwalking has been identified with female sexual repression, thus it is not surprising that in Sheridan Le Fanu's "Carmilla"; and Bram Stoker's *Dracula*, women are subjected to hypnotic/sleepwalking activity. Hysteria is manifested through the act of sleepwalking, to symbolize transgressions within society and the self. Although melodrama is a genre which aims to excite the audience through incident; it is a genre which depicts extremities. Extremities play an important role in relation to sleepwalking, as it questions the ability for one to transgress boundaries. As Peter Brooks states:

> Melodrama is a drama of "excess" in which life choices seem finally to have little to do with the surface realities of a situation and much more to do with an intense inner drama of consciousness and a manichaestic struggle of good and evil[20]

Le Fanu and Stoker put into play a range of contemporary fears and fantasises about modernity, class, empire, sex and sexuality. Carmilla, Dracula and Lucy transgress as individuals between life and death, man/monster, woman/cat, woman/vampire, past and present and east and west. In "Le Horla", the state of hypnotism/trance plays a key role in relation to the narrator's unstable identity. In "Le Horla", questions regarding the self are raised, as it is perceived to be destructive to the narrator. Hence, the act of sleepwalking in these three texts does not simply raise concerns of female subject positions, but also the instability and transgression of identity.

Le Fanu originally published "Carmilla" in the short lived Victorian periodical *The Dark Blue*, and included the tale *In a Glass Darkly*. "Carmilla" focuses on women's attempt to usurp patriarchal power. This is demonstrated through two strong relationships: through the union between Carmilla and her mother and secondly by the alliance between Carmilla and Laura. Interestingly, it is Carmilla, the vampire who appears to be the somnambulist in this novella:

---

[20] Peter Brooks, *The Melodramatic: Imagination, Balzac, Henry James, Melodrama and the Mode of Excess (New York: Columbia University Press,* 1984), p.12.

'It was past two last night', she said, 'when I went to sleep as usual in my bed, with my doors locked, that of the dressing room, and that opening upon the gallery. My sleep was uninterrupted, and, so far, as I know, dreamless; but I woke just now on the sofa in the dressing room there, and I found the door between the rooms open, and the other door forced. How could all this have happened without my being wakened?'[21]

When Carmilla is questioned by Laura's father about any subsequent sleepwalking activity, she responds: 'Never, since I was very young indeed'. Secondly, in chapter thirteen, entitled 'The Woodman', Laura describes Carmilla as:

Walking through the trees, in an easterly direction, and looking like a person in trance. How did she pass out from her room, leaving the door locked on the inside? How did she escape from the house without unbarring the window? (p.78)

Sleepwalking or the act of sleepwalking is a device used by Carmilla to execute her vampiric intentions. Carmilla is not the victim, she is the victimizer. It is Carmilla who places Laura under some form of trance, which 'draws me (Laura) to her':

Her murmured words sounded like a lullaby in my ears, and soothed my resistance into a trance, from which I only seemed to recover when she withdrew her arms. (p.34)

The significance of sleepwalking in this text is the way in which the characters who encounter Carmilla, are unconsciously drawn to her and are oblivious to her as a threat to society and themselves. It is not until the end of the narrative, that the characters are made aware that Carmilla / Millarca is in fact a vampire. On a broader scale, the importance this has is that it demonstrates the incompetence of men such as Laura's father and General Spielsdorf to fulfil their duties as father/protector.

---

[21] Sheridan Le Fanu, "Carmilla" (France: Zulma Classics, 2005), p.57. All further references to this text are given parenthetically in the dissertation

General Spielsdorf, like Laura's father is duped by Carmilla's mother, by submitting to:

> The charms of sex and rank by convincing himself that Millarca's mother was throwing herself entirely upon my chivalry... She in some sort disarmed me... quite overpowered, I submitted'. (p.74)

The diction that General Spielsdorf uses seems to parody that of a battle taking place between Carmilla's mother and himself. He uses the words 'disarmed me', 'overpowered' and 'submitted', which suggests that masculinity is weak in the face of female sexuality. The point that Le Fanu is putting forward here is if Carmilla and her mother are able to take take advantage of Ruskin's doctrine of 'separate spheres'. Ruskin's ideology depicts women as the repositories of innocence and order, who require protection from the male gender as the male gender is nobler and stronger. Man, Ruskin claims:

> Active, progressive, defensive... Eminently the doer, the creator, the discoverer, the defender... Woman is enduringly, incorruptibly, good; instinctively, infallibly wise... not for self-development, but for self-renunciation. (p.310)

The flaw in Ruskin's thoughts is that he fails to recognize not all women are incorruptible and not all men are strong and noble. If anything, this text shows how men are passive and unable to shield their daughter/niece from harm. For instance, on the evening Carmilla disappears from the schloss, Laura and her maids are said to become:

> Frightened... [and] rang the bell long and furiously. If my father's room had been at that side of the house, we would have called him up at once to our aid. But alas! He was quite out of hearing and to reach him involved an excursion. (p.54)

The only resolution available to Laura is 'to cool a little and soon recovered [her] senses sufficiently to dismiss the men'. Another occurrence of male frailty is General Spielsdorf's unsuccessful attempt to capture Carmilla. He tells Laura:

> I saw a large black object, very ill-defined, crawl, as it seemed to me, over the foot of the bed, and swiftly spread itself up to the poor girl's throat... I stood petrified. I now sprang forward, with my sword in hand... I struck at her instantly with my sword; but I saw her standing near the door, unscathed. I pursued, and struck again she was gone! And my sword flew into shivers against the door. (p.85)

General Spielsdorf's 'sword' is a metaphor of his masculinity, fails him when he encounters Carmilla. Carmilla is able to escape Spielsdorf's attempts to annihilate her; instead it is she who diminishes his power: 'my sword flew into shivers'. Essentially, the danger in this novella is not so much Carmilla, but the lack of male authority and stability at home. Fred Botting subscribes to this view as he states:

> The absence of a stable paternal order provides room for the projection of both ideal and terrifying figures of authority and power. These substitute fathers indicate the familial, religious and social institutions threatened by moral and paternal decline[22]

The fact that Laura's father remains anonymous throughout the whole narrative re-emphasizes not only his detachment from his household, but also the insignificance of a male presence.

The fact that Carmilla and her mother prey on Bertha and Laura (who are both motherless), implies that it is the mother, not father who protects the domestic sphere. Russel M. Goldfarb states this idea in *Sexual Repression and Victorian Literature*:

> The Victorian woman had a constant role to play as moral guardian of her society, her relations, and her home. She stabilized the Victorian family, which was the single most important unit in preserving the order of nineteenth century England.[23]

---

[22] Fred Botting, "Aftergothic: consumption, machines and black holes", in *The Cambridge Companion to Gothic Fiction,* ed. Jerrold E. Hogle (Cambridge: Cambridge University Press, 2002), p.284.

[23] Russel M. Goldfarb, *Sexual Repression and Victorian Literature* (Bucknell: Bucknell University Press, 1975), p. 10.

If the mother is an important entity in the Victorian household, then it easy to understand why Laura and Carmilla seek solace in one another. Even though Carmilla has preyed on girls other than Laura, it is evident that she is attached to Laura. Carmilla first comes to Laura when she is six years old:

> I saw a solemn, but very pretty face looking at me from the side of the bed. It was that of a young lady who was kneeling, with her hands under the coverlet. I looked at her with a kind of pleased wonder, and ceased whimpering. She caressed me with her hands, and lay down beside me on the bed, and drew me towards her, smiling. I felt immediately delightfully soothed, and fell asleep again. I was wakened by a sensation as if 2 needles ran into my breast very deep at the same moment, and I cried loudly. (p.15)

Carmilla's behaviour is overtly sexual, as suggested by the diction: 'caressed', 'hands under the coverlet' and 'drew me towards her'. However, Carmilla's actions can also be read as a need for love, not necessarily something sexual. Even though Carmilla has a mother; she does not play an active role in Carmilla's life, in the way that she leaves Carmilla in strange households. This idea is present in Bram Stoker's *Dracula*, whereby both Lucy and Mina (who are motherless), have a strong friendship. Some critics have considered their relationship to be indirectly sexual as Lucy writes to Mina: 'I wish I were with you, dear, sitting by the fire undressing' (p.55). It is simple to read both friendships as sexual, however from what has been discussed about the role of the mother, it seems as though these friendships are concerned with filling a void, which neither father nor husband can do. The friendship between Carmilla and Laura is more to do with female solidarity, within a patriarchal environment. Laura welcomes Carmilla's friendship because Carmilla stands for freedom.

From the very beginning of the novella, Laura tells the reader 'my gouvernantes had just so much control over me as you might control' (p.15). The tone in which Laura says 'so much control over me', is one of resentment; as her upbringing entails that she be under strict discipline. What makes Laura's words interesting is that she uses the adverb 'so', which illustrates the extent to which she feels suffocated in her surroundings. This perhaps can explain why Laura gravitates towards Carmilla. Throughout the text, Carmilla is presented as an unrestricted woman in the way that she speaks and the way she is able to escape from the schloss. An example of Carmilla's lack of restraint is in the way Le Fanu presents the newly restored Karnstein family portraits. After unveiling one portrait dated 1698 and bearing the name Marcia Karnstein, Laura exclaims 'it was quite beautiful; it was startling; it seemed to live. It was the effigy of Carmilla!' (p.43). What makes this portrait noteworthy is that the picture is presented 'without a frame', which reflects Carmilla's rampant sexuality. In *The Flesh Made Word,* Helen Michie concludes that:

> Frequently women characters are distanced from their lovers and their readers by appearing as either texts or works (objects) of art… The act of unframing oneself, of stepping out of one's portrait, is a subversive and dangerous move for women.[24]

Like the unframed Karnstein portrait, the entire 'Carmilla' narrative is incompletely framed. In the prologue to the text, the editor comments:

> Upon a paper attached to the narrative which follows, Doctor Hesselius has written a rather elaborate note, which he accompanies with a reference to his essay on the strange subject which the Ms. Illuminates.

Ironically, the narrative ends without presenting either Doctor Hesselius' excerpt or the editor's comments.

Even though Carmilla is vanquished, female power is nonetheless asserted by Laura. It is Laura, not Carmilla who demonstrates her lack of restraint as she chooses to disregard any male contribution to her story, and addresses the narrative to a 'town lady like you' (p.35). This example relates to what was discussed earlier on about Carmilla and Laura's relationship to be more concerned with female unity and the capability for a woman to express herself. Despite the passage of time, Carmilla's memory is prominent in Laura's life:

---

[24] Helen Michie, *The Flesh Made Word: Female Figures and Women's Bodies* (Oxford: Oxford University Press, 1987), p.107.

> To this hour, the image of Carmilla returns to memory with ambiguous alternations——sometimes the playful, languid, beautiful, sometimes the writhing fiend I saw in the ruined church; and often from a reverie I have started, fancying I heard the light step of Carmilla at the drawing room door. (p.95)

If evil has been destroyed then its legacy has not. Laura's final words are unquestionably ambiguous. Laura's language mirrors the state of sleepwalker, in the way that her mind is in turmoil over the way she feels about Carmilla. On the one hand, she consciously sees Carmilla as a 'writhing fiend', but at the same time, there is an underlying desire for Carmilla to return. This reflects Laura's confused mind between what she consciously feels and a repressed feeling for Carmilla to re-enter her life. Elizabeth Signorotti acknowledges the vague conclusion of the text:

> The conclusion of Laura's narrative confirms the reader's suspicions that everything Carmilla represents, if not Carmilla herself, remains loose and desirable in Styria[25]

If Le Fanu frees his female characters from subject positions in patriarchal society; Bram Stoker decidedly returns women in the social system, whereby he punishes Lucy for subverting social morals and presents Mina as the ideal female paradigm. It is worth mentioning Stoker's psychology before he came to write Dracula, in order to understand why Stoker was pre-occupied with the representation of 'good' and 'bad' women. The basis of Stoker's struggle with female sexuality can be traced to his relationship with his wife. In 1878 Stoker married Florence Balcombe, who one year later gave birth to their son, Noel. It was understood by Stoker's granddaughter that after the birth of Noel, sexual intimacy between the couple had ceased. By not submitting herself sexually to Bram, Florence was not fulfilling her duty as wife. Ergo, in creating *Dracula*, Stoker placed the women, firmly under male control. Like "Carmilla", sleepwalking in *Dracula* is a mode through which Stoker voices his apprehension of women

---

[25] Elizabeth Signorotti, *"Repossessing the body: transgressive desire in 'Carmilla' and Dracula- Vampire story retold with masculine themes added"*. September 22, 1996. http://www.findarticles/lit/elizabethsignorotti.

and familial stability. The central anxiety of this novel is the battle of the son (symbolized by the Crew of Light); against the father (Dracula) to release the desired woman, the mother. Richardson comments:

> The set-up reminds one rather of the primal horde as pictured somewhat fantastically perhaps by Freud in *Totem and Taboo*, with the brothers bonding together against the father who has tried to keep all the females to himself[26]

Having said that, the novel affirms a pre-oedipal concern. In other words, fear not so much of the father but the mother, who is represented by Lucy and Mina. In the former, the mother is more desirable, more sexual, more threatening and as a result she must be destroyed. Mina on the other hand, is saved because she follows the Symbolic Order by submitting herself to the Crew of Light and assisting them in their attempts to locate Dracula.

Lucy embodies aspects of the New Woman, who rejects conventional female modes and demands sexual and social autonomy, which is punished in this novel. Female vampires like Carmilla, represent a rejection of maternity in their preference not for feeding but rather feeding on others. This is exhibited in Castle Dracula, whereby the vampires and subsequently Lucy, reject the woman's central role as mother and caregiver:

> With a careless motion, she [Lucy] flung to the ground, callous as a devil, the child that up to now she had clutched strenuously to her breast growing over it as a dog growls over a bone. The child gave a sharp cry, and lay there moaning.[27]

What is particularly disturbing about Lucy is the manner in which her sexual desires emerge with her transformation. The reader is made aware of Lucy's sexual nature earlier on in the novel as she flirts overtly with her three suitors and remarks: 'Why can't they let a girl marry three men, or

---

[26] Maurice Richardson, 'The Psychoanalysis of Ghost Stories', *Twentieth Century*, 166 (December 1959), p.28.
[27] Bram Stoker, *Dracula* (Oxford: Oxford University Press, 1998), p.211. All further references to this text are given parenthetically in the dissertation.

as many as want her, and save all this trouble?' (p. 59). In psychoanalytic terms, vampirism is a disguise for greatly desired and equally feared desires; in the same way that sleepwalking in "Carmilla" is a disguise for Carmilla to leave the schloss. Vampirism in "Carmilla" and *Dracula* represents individual freedom: with Laura it is freedom from her governesses and with Lucy it is sexual freedom.

Some critics adopt the view that Dracula's Call of Death places Lucy under a trance to seduce her. This is true, however, when Mina describes Lucy's absence from the bedroom; there is a sense that Lucy is not hypnotized into vampirism, but willingly submits herself to it:

> The room was dark, so I could not see Lucy's bed; I stole across and felt for her. The bed was empty. I lit a match, and found that she was not in the room. As I was leaving the room it struck me that the clothes she wore might give me some clue to her dreaming intention. Dressing gown would mean house; dress, outside. (p.89)

Lucy's clothes are not only a clue to Mina but also to the reader. Lucy sleepwalks in her dressing gown, unlike her father who would 'get up in the night and dress himself' (p.72), whilst he sleepwalked out of his room. This image of Lucy wearing her dressing gown indicates the ease in which she can express herself and her sexuality, without having to repress or constrain it in the form of dress.

Once Lucy embraces vampirism, her physical description demonstrates the way in which she has transgressed. When Dr. Seward first sees Lucy, he describes her hair 'in its usual sunny ripples' (p.60), later on when the men watch her as a vampire returning to her tomb, Lucy is described as a 'dark haired woman' (p.210). Thus, the state of sleepwalking expresses binary oppositions within the novel such as: normal/abnormal, sensuality/passivity and life/death. Another example of binary opposition is the way that the state of death can generate life. For example, Lucy's split-self or 'unconscious cerebration' (p.270) when she sleepwalks is very peculiar. Whilst she sleepwalks, Lucy is said to have an 'anaemic look' and is 'pale' (p.109); this is juxtaposed to death restoring 'part of her beauty', which makes Lucy a 'very beautiful corpse' (p.162). Once death has set in, the earliest self-division now articulates itself in an uncanny representation of her previous beauty, against the natural process of 'decay's effacing fingers' (p.164). 'Every hour' according to Seward, 'seemed to be enhancing her loveliness' (p.168). The duplicity of Lucy's body just after sleepwalking transfers her from one phallocentric power to another. The difference between the two male powers is that one seeks to repress sexual desire, whereas vampirism seeks to express it.

The only interactions which are sexualized in this novel are those between humans and vampires, which is a deliberate attempt to portray sexuality as unthinkable in 'normal' male/female relationships. For example, when Jonathan Harker searches Castle Dracula, he encounters three vampires:

> All three had brilliant white teeth that shone like pearls against the ruby of their voluptuous lips. There was something about them that made me uneasy, some longing at the same time deadly fear. I felt in my heart a wicked, burning desire that they would kiss me with those red lips. P.47.

It is not surprising that Harker feels 'desire' for the female vampires because in his 'normal' world, Mina who is the ideal, subordinate woman is sexless. The vampires evoke Harker's repressed desire that 'they would kiss me with those red lips'. Another example is the scene in which Dracula slits open his breast and forces Mina Harker to drink his blood, which is allegorical to oral fellatio:

> With his left hand he held both Mrs. Harker's hands, keeping them away with her arms at full tension; his right hand gripped her by the back of the neck, forcing her face down on his bosom. Her white nightdress was smeared with blood... The attitude of the two had a terrible resemblance to a child forcing a kitten's nose into a saucer of milk to compel to drink. (p.313)

These two examples show that the marriage between Jonathan and Mina is asexual in contrast to these two incidents of lust and passion. These two scenes also portray two levels of the self, in the same way that Lucy's hair mirrors two levels of consciousness. These scenes show that

Jonathan and Mina's union is respectable because it is not based on lust, whereas vampirism is not associated with love, but with fulfilling of desire. Stoker himself said:

> A close analysis will show that the only emotions which in the long run harm are those arising from sex impulses, and when we have realised this we have put a finger on the actual point of danger.[28]

Obviously, it would have been complicated for Stoker to overtly portray sex or acts of a sexual nature in this novel, considering the context it was written in. Alternatively, Stoker employs the use of blood to equate it with sperm and intercourse. The Sanguine Economy, in the nineteenth century was regarded as a counterpart to the Spermatic Economy. The Spermatic economy was a quasi-medical discourse, in which semen was regarded as a product of the blood. In both economies, there was a relationship between a bodily fluid, such as blood or semen. Edward Bliss Foote explains this concept:

> When semen is discharged or 'spent', the consequent generation of fresh spermatozoa draws from the blood all its purest and most strengthening qualities; leaving the patient drained and exhausted.[29]

One such example of this in the novel is when Lucy who becomes a vampire in the Hampstead churchyard, is described:

> With a languorous, voluptuous grace, said: 'come to me, Arthur. Leave these others and come to me. My arms are hungry for you. Come, and we can rest together. Come my husband, come! (p.258)

Lucy is 'hungry' for both blood and sperm. In order to obtain sperm from Arthur, Lucy needs to extract his blood. Furthermore, in an attempt to cure Lucy of her wild sexuality, Van Helsing and his crew of 'brave

---

[28] Daniel Farson, *The man who wrote Dracula: A biography of Bram Stoker* (London: Michael Joseph, 1975), p.22.
[29] Edward Bliss Foote, *Home Cyclopedia of Popular Medical, Social and Sexual Science* (London: L.N. Fowler, 1901), p.167.

men' (p.234), perform four major blood transfusions on her. The act of transfusing blood, of penetrating Lucy's body with the phallic needle and enabling the men to deposit their own fluids in her, conjures up an image of gang rape, as Lucy is restricted on her bed.

Ironically, Lucy's wish to marry 'as many men' (p.59), violently comes true in this very scene. This is because each transfusion which takes place signifies the consummation of four marriages between Lucy and Arthur, Quincey Morris, Van Helsing and Seward. The four blood transfusions which take place, forces Van Helsing to comment that 'this so sweet maid is a polyandrist' (p.176). Finally, after staking and beheading Lucy, the candle which the men hold is said to 'drop white patches' on Lucy's coffin. The 'white patches' can be read as a metaphor for sperm. Once the 'sperm' has come into contact with Lucy, she is described as 'shook and quivered and twisted in violent contortions'. Once penetration has taken place, Lucy is no longer seen as a 'foul thing':

> There in the coffin lay no longer the foul thing which we had so dreaded and grown to hate that the work of her destruction was yielded to the one best entitled to it, but Lucy as we had seen her in her life, with her face of unequalled sweetness and purity. (p.259)

This quotation seems to infer that the female body politic is on constant display for men to view. It seems to be clear, as the novel progresses, Stoker is not simply interested in depicting sex or sexuality through the metaphor of blood. Stoker is concerned with Lucy and Mina's bodies. Like the act of sleepwalking, Lucy and Mina are unconsciously aware that for men to control them, they need to posses their bodies. Throughout the novel, different forms of media are used to communicate information such as letters script, typewriting, hypnotism and wax cylinders to receive voice impressions. Thus, the novel is occupied with eclectic forms of marking or inscribing on so many different surfaces. The effect this has is that it gives whoever is marking or inscribing, possession of their narrative and voice.

In order for men to possess women in this novel, they too need to mark them. Dale Spender has observed, under patriarchy, 'masculinity is always the unmarked form and femininity the marked'[30]. Lucy's body is a centre

---

[30] Dale Spender, *Man Made Language* (London: Faber, 1985), p.20.

for male possession and control. Lucy's body is owned by Dracula, who leaves bite scars on her neck and at the same time; the Crew of Light leave red bruises on her arm, as a result from the blood transfusions. Rebecca A. Pope recognizes this theme of inscription and claiming of the female body as a form of control:

> The staking of Lucy, a marking of the female body that simultaneously punishes and reclaims the woman who transgresses the traditional code of feminine behaviour[31]

Dracula, the father of vampirism competes against Van Helsing the father of the Crew of Light in possessing Lucy and Mina. Dracula possesses Lucy by leaving bite marks on her; Van Helsing touches a host to Mina's forehead, burning her (p.316), which can symbolically be interpreted as her catharsis from vampirism. Mina's body like her personality is subservient to Van Helsing and the other men. It is Mina who tells Van Helsing 'you can hypnotize me and so learn that which even I myself do not know' (p.311). Mina offers her supine, hypnotized and passive body for the men to explore. This links into the idea of Mina being the ideal woman, as it is she who feeds the men information about Dracula. This is set side by side with Lucy's body, which is a site of sexual prey and lust, whereby she takes the group's blood. In contrast, Mina's body transmits messages from Dracula directly to the men, after waking she has 'no recollection of what has passed'.

Mina is Lucy's döppelgänger, who is the model woman/wife/mother. Mina undergoes the same near death experiences as her deceased friend; Mina is bitten in her sleep and has the same visions and symptoms as Lucy:

> I didn't know that she was here till se spoke; and she didn't look the same. I don't care for the pale people; I like them with lots of blood in them and hers all seemed to have run out... He had been taking life out of her. (p.320)

The difference between Mina and Lucy is that Lucy does not tell anyone about her sleepwalking experiences. Mina says that 'she did not

---

[31] Rebecca A. Pope, *Writing and Biting in Dracula*, LIT, 1 (1990), P.206.

speak, even when she wrote that which she wished to be known later' (p.323). *Au contraire*, Mina is clearly on the side of the paternal law. She tells Van Helsing of her experiences, and is able to help him with documentation. In other words, what makes Mina the model of femininity is that she is supportive and at the same time submissive. Elizabeth Bronfen supports this view:

> Mina relates her near death experiences to the vampire hunters and is a seminal accomplice in their search. Unlike Lucy, whose desire for death is coterminous with an insecurity about her status as a bride, she accepts her fixture within the Symbolic Order and resists the call of death, despite her initial response to it[32]

Mina, like Lucy, embodies traits associated with the New Woman. It is her intelligence not her licentiousness which is drawn to the readers attention. Van Helsing observes that 'wonderful maiden Mina', has a 'man's brain – a brain that a man should have were he gifted' (p.340). Mina's intelligence is illustrated in the way she transcribes events in shorthand and types them in order to help the men with their documentation. Mina's intelligence can only be exercised to a certain extent whilst the vampire hunt takes place. Van Helsing tells Jonathan Harker that it is 'no part for a woman... her heart may fail her' (p.324). Mina, unlike Lucy, does not resist but succumbs to male authority, which makes her a 'sweet, sweet, good, good woman'; and ends the novel as the 'brave and gallant mother', full of 'sweetness and loving care' (p.308).

"Le Horla" is one of Maupassant's most complex *contes fantastiques*. The story focuses on the psychology of the individual and develops the notion of an internal döppelgänger. Like "Carmilla" and *Dracula*, this tale presents binaries as a central feature of duality within the individual: darkness/light, emptiness/fullness, visibility/invisibility, open/closed, sanity/madness and self/other. The themes in "Le Horla" are different to those in "Carmilla" and Dracula. "Le Horla" is not preoccupied with women or female sexuality, but is concerned with the narrator's identity and the battle between reality and fantasy. "Le Horla" is a convoluted

---

[32] Elizabeth Bronfen, *Over Her Dead Body: Death, Femininity and the Aesthetic* (Manchester: Manchester University Press, 1992), p.313.

story which raises many unanswered questions: 'is Le Horla a feminine spirit?' and 'does the spirit haunt the narrator? Or is it a figment of his imagination?' Whatever the answers are to these questions, what can be said about this novella is that it explores the boundaries between reality and fantasy. Maupassant seems to be interested in the narrator's response to the amalgamation of reality and the supernatural. Tzvetan Todorov states that:

> The fantastic is that hesitation experienced by a person who knows only the laws of nature, confronting an apparently supernatural event[33]

What links "Le Horla" with "Carmilla" and *Dracula*, is that sleepwalking is used as a device to depict the collision of two models of reality. These two modes of reality are the incursion of extra-normal events, into the everyday world, which challenge social/moral boundaries and the ability to transgress these boundaries. Kelly Hurley argues this idea in her discussion of the fantastic:

> The character's panicked inability to interpret the strange event-lets us know we have breached the knowledge of systems of the text's culture, thus allowing us to determine where normal realities end and alternate or impossible realities begin for that culture[34]

Le Horla comes to the narrator at night whilst he is sleeping. The way that the spirit is described is somewhat similar to that of Carmilla's entrance into Laura's bedroom:

---

[33] Tzvetan Todorov, *The Fantastic: a structural approach to a literary genre* (Ithaca: Cornell University Press, 1975), p.25.

[34] Kelly Hurley, "British Gothic Fiction, 1885-1930", in *The Cambridge Companion to Gothic Fiction*, ed. Jerrold E. Hogle (Cambridge: Cambridge University Press, 2002), p.204.

> Cette nuit, j'ai senti quelqu'un accroupi sur moi, et qui, sa bouche sur la mienne, buvait ma vie entre mes lèvres. Oui, il la puisait dans ma gorge, comme aurait fait une sangsue[35]

The quotation implies that Le Horla is not a spirit, but a vampire in the way that 'he was sucking all of my neck'. Once Le Horla presents itself as a threat to the narrator, he begins to lose his grasp of reality. This is implied in the way that the narrator has no jurisdiction over his speech or actions. This is evident when the narrator suspects himself of sleepwalking:

> J'étais somnambule, je vivais, sans le savoir, de cette double vie mystérieuse qui fait douter s'il y a deux êtres en nous[36] (p. 17/18)

As the story progresses, the reader is made aware that the narrator is not a somnambulist, but is placed under the influence by some 'other' being:

> Je suis perdu! Quelq'un possède mon âme et la gouverne! Quelq'un ordonne tous mes actes, tous mes mouvements, toutes mes pensées. Je ne suis plus rien en moi, rien qu'un spectateur esclave et terrifié de toutes les chose que j'accomplis[37] (p.33)

The same conflicts which arise in "Carmilla" and *Dracula* are present in this text. On the one hand, Le Horla wants to possess and claim the narrator. On the other, the narrator consistently attempts to reassert his identity: 's'enfermer mon image'. The constant use of mirrors and looking at oneself at the mirror, reinforces the narrator's need to regain his sense of self, which Le Horla undermines:

---

[35] Last night I felt somebody leaning on me who was sucking my life from between my lips with his mouth. Yes, he was sucking all of my neck, like a leach would have done. *Guy de Maupassant, 'Le Horla'* (Paris: Libraire Générale Française, 1976), p16. All further references to this text are given parenthetically in the dissertation.

[36] I was a somnambulist. I lived without knowing it, that double mysterious life which makes us doubt whether there are not two beings in us.

[37] I am lost! Somebody possesses my soul and governs it! Somebody orders all my acts, all my movements, all my thoughts. I am no longer anything in myself, nothing except an enslaved and terrified spectator of all things which I do.

> On y voyait comme en plein jour, et je ne me vis pas dans ma glace! Elle était vide, claire, profonde, pleine de lumière! Mon image n'était pas dedans...et j'étais en face, moi![38] (p.43)

The irony is that Le Horla who is invisible, absorbs the reflection of a living man. This reinforces the idea that the story is interested with dispossession of the narrator by an external force. The hypnotism of Mme Sablé by Doctor Parent is important, as it expands the theme of lost identity. Mme Sablé like Le Horla is able to create the narrator's reflection by using the visiting-card:

> <<Mettez-vous derrière elle>>, dit le médecin. Et je m'assis derrière elle. Il lui plaça entre les mains une carte de visite en lui disant: <<Ceci est un mirror; que voyez-vous dedans?>>
> Elle répondit:
> <<Je vous mon cousin>>[39] (p.23)

It is the 'other' in this tale that can see and control the narrator's reflection/self. Evidently this shows the narrator's weakening self power. The fact that he is unable to destroy Le Horla without destroying his house implies that this monster is not inside his home, but in his mind. This follows the narrator's eventual downfall: <<Il va donc falloir que je me tue moi>> (p.47)[40]. From what has been discussed, trance is used as a device to repress and destroy the individual. Vampires are used in "Carmilla" and *Dracula* to represent the state of otherness/repressed desire, however in "Le Horla"; it is not a vampire who is destructive, but the human mind.

---

[38] It was as bright as midday, hut I did not see myself in the glass! It was empty, clear, profound, full of light! But my figure was not reflected in it... and I, I was opposite to it!

[39] "Stand behind her," the doctor said to me, and so I took a seat behind her. He put a visiting-card into her hands, and said to her: 'This is a looking-glass; what do you see in it?' And she replied: 'I see my cousin'

[40] 'I suppose I must kill myself!'

'Britain is Sleepwalking into Hell's Pit' Sleepwalking & the State

In this chapter, sleepwalking will be discussed as a way to represent the decline of Britain as an imperialist country and post war Germany. Furthermore, sleepwalking will be examined in relation to the hypnotic relationship between leader and crowd, in Gustave Le Bon's *Crowd Psychology*.

In Arthur Conan Doyle's 1887 story *A Study in Scarlet*, Dr. Watson states:

> I naturally gravitated to London, that great cesspool into which all the loungers and idlers of the Empire are irresistibly drained[41]

Dr. Watson's comment that London is 'drained' from the 'loungers and idlers of the Empire' reflects the general attitude that many had about Britain's empire and its people. The reason why Britons in the nineteenth century had a pessimistic view about the east is because:

> [It was] linked thus to elements in western society (delinquents, the insane, women, the poor) having in common an identity best described as alien. Orientals were rarely seen or looked at; they were seen through, analysed not as citizens[42]

---

[41] Arthur Conan Doyle, A Study in Scarlet (Oxford: Oxford University Press, 1993), p.6.
[42] Edward Said, *Orientalism* (London: Routledge, 1978), p.207.

Contrary to the views upheld by Dr. Watson and his contemporaries, Britain, specifically London, was a place of decadence, disease and degeneration during the 1880's and 1890's. In 1888, *The Lancet* published an article entitled "Are we degenerating physically?" which describes degeneration in England as:

> Undoubtedly at work among town-bred populations as the consequence of wholesome occupations, improper [diet] and juvenile vice... While the optimistic view has most to urge in its favour, it would be wrong to ignore the existence of widespread evils and serious dangers to the public health. Amongst these evils and dangers are enumerated sexual indulgence in early life, premature marriages, over-pressure in education, improper food, increased tension... and the abuse of alcohol and tobacco[43]

W.T.Stead, a contemporary editor went further to remark that Britain was 'sleepwalking into hell's pit'[44]. Stead's comment seems to suggest that Britain was unconscious of its moral and physical downfall. In *Dracula* and *The Moonstone*, Britain is presented as both the invader and a city of invasion. In both texts, Britain is depicted as a place of chaos and anarchy.

In *Dracula*, Britain's diminishing power is emblematized through the characterization of Lucy. Lucy's surname 'Westenra' is important because it suggests that Lucy symbolizes the west. The fact that Lucy is possessed by Dracula and subsequently becomes a 'citizen' of vampirism, emphasizes Britain's weakening power. Elizabeth Lynn Linton agrees with this viewpoint:

> Lucy's surname is significant, in infecting this synecdoche of the British race, Dracula is not only colonising the west, but also modifying its cultural identity by sapping its moral and physical energy as presented through Lucy[45]

---

[43] "Are we degenerating physically?", *The Lancet*, Vol. 2, 1888, 1,076.
[44] http://www.alangullette.com/lit/shiel/essays/shiel_stead.htm. Website accessed on May 3, 2005.
[45] Elizabeth Lynn Linton, "The girl of the period", *The Girl of the Period and other Social Essays*, (London: Bentley, 1883), vol.1, p.1.

Furthermore, the disparity between Dracula's control over the main characters and their lack of mental autonomy is consistent throughout the text. Mina's account of Lucy's seduction in the grounds of the Abbey gives details of the 'long and black' figure, with a 'white face and red gleaming eyes' (p.90). Harker states: 'I felt myself struggling to awake some call of my instincts… I was becoming hypnotized' (p.44). Similarly, Mina states 'I was bewildered, and strangely enough, I did not want to hinder him' (p.287). Lord Godalming describes the situation as 'hysterical' and even Van Helsing who is 'one of the most advanced scientists of the day'; (p.112) becomes 'disturbed'. Seward records how in the face of Lucy's death, Van Helsing becomes hysterical:

> He gave way to a regular fit of hysterics… He laughed till he cried and I had to draw the blinds lest anyone should see us and misjudge. (P.174)

These citations show how everyone in the text calls into question his/her mental status, which suggests an anxiety about their environment which is being invaded. These examples say something of the British race and Britain's declining power, towards the end of the nineteenth century. Paul Kennedy observes that between 1885-1918:

> Britain's relative share of world production steadily diminished and in the newer and increasingly more important industries such as steel, chemicals, machine tools, and electrical goods, Britain soon lost what early lead it possessed[46]

Britain's declining power is pertinent in Stoker's novel, where he makes reference to the shift in international power from England to America. This is asserted by Renfield, who tells Quincey:

> Mr. Morris, you should be proud of your great state. Its reception into the Union was a precedent which may have far-reaching effects hereafter, when the Pole and the Tropics may hold allegiance to the

---

[46] Paul Kennedy, *The Rise and Fall of the Great Powers: economic change and military conflict from c. 1500-c.2000* (New York: Random House, 1987), p.228.

Stars and Stripes. The power of the Treaty may yet prove a vast engine of enlargement, when the Monroe doctrine takes its true place as a political fable. (P.291)

Images of decline and potential disaster are presented throughout the text, which re-emphasizes Stoker's anxiety about Britain disintegration. For instance Dracula's castle is said to be located 'on the very edge of a terrible precipice' (p.38). When Dracula comes to London, he lodges in a 'partially ruined building' which is 'surrounded by a high wall, of ancient structure... that had not been repaired for years' (p.119). Finally, the ship Demeter is said to be 'drifting to some terrible doom' (p.105).

In *The Moonstone*, Rachel Verinder is a character which Collins uses as a means of conveying the theme of colonization. Rachel's dark features, underscores her likeness to the Indians: 'Her hair was the blackest I ever saw. Her eyes matched her hair' (p.58). Like Britain's overseas colonies, femininity too is a dark continent which needs to be explored and possessed. Rachel's likening to the Indians says something about the way that Britain needs to explore people and colonies and that both women and Britain's colonies need to be better understood. It is worth cross-referencing to Collins' other text "Who Killed Zebedee?" as the same idea is put forward. As the investigation progresses into who killed Zebedee, the irony is that the inspector suspects Mr. Deluc, a 'Creole gentleman' (p.9) as the murderer. Upon the first encounter with Mr. Deluc, the speaker's description is animates:

> He was wrapped in a splendid blue dressing-gown, with a golden girdle and trimmings... His complexion was yellow. His greenish-brown eyes were of the sort called 'goggle'- they looked as if they might drop out of this face if you held a spoon under them. (P.12)

There is something almost unearthly in the way that the speaker describes Mr. Deluc. The references to different colours: 'blue dressing gown', 'golden girdle', 'yellow' and greenish-brown' create a distorted picture of the man. The tone that the speaker uses to describe Mr Deluc implies that he is someone who is 'different', in the way that he says his eyes were a 'sort' called 'goggle'. The use of the word 'sort' suggests another type of human species, a species which is not English.

Collins uses Mr. Deluc to critique the way that the inspector fully questions him, and not any other member of the household. It is Mr. Deluc's foreign exterior which automatically incriminates him as the speaker says that, the inspector would 'question this witness sharply and closely':

> He [the inspector] was not a man to be misled by appearances but I could see that he was far from liking, or even trusting Mr. Deluc. (P.12)

The speaker's words are absolutely preposterous if not banal. The inspector and the speaker are both 'misled' by appearances from the very moment they entered Mrs Crosscapel's lodging house. The inspector has no evidence against Mr Deluc to suspect him of murder, but the reason why he dislikes the man is because he is a foreigner. The inspector takes the trouble of delving into Mr Deluc's past, but fails to do the same with any other person residing in the house:

> We found Deluc to have led a dissipated life, and to have mixed with very bad company. But he kept out of reach of the law. (p.19).

The example of Mr Deluc re-emphasizes the idea that Britain needs to explore women and its colonies because what is implied from "Who Killed Zebedee?" is that appearances deceive, which allows someone like Priscilla to get away with murder.

In *The Moonstone*, Britain's double-standard is emblematized by the use of the opium. Opium is used to induce Franklin Blake's sleepwalking by Mr. Candy and Ezra Jennings. The effect that opium has upon Franklin Blake is that it exposes his repressed motives and desires. Once Blake awakens, he is in a state of oblivion as to what events have passed in his act of sleepwalking. This seems to suggest that Britain is like Blake, unconscious of what is taking place in India. Gail Marshall discuses this in her argument:

> Opium acts metonymically to suggest a whole society operating in wilful ignorance of its own doubleness, as it acted in wilful ignorance of the imperial activities and atrocities upon which domestic prosperity rested[47]

In this text, opium is connected with Ezra Jennings, who like Mr Deluc is an outsider in his society. Ezra Jennings, like Rosanna is a tragic figure who lives on the margins of Victorian society. His strange appearance seems to define him for others and encourage their social rejection of him:

> His complexion was of gypsy darkness; his fleshless cheeks had fallen into deep hollows, over which the bone projected like a penthouse. His nose presented the fine shape and modelling so often found among the ancient people of the East… At one place, the white hair ran up into the black; at another, the black hair ran down into the white. (P.358/9)

The same juxtapositions that Collins used to describe Blake at the Shivering Sand are used here to portray Jennings. Otherness in the form of the East is manifested in Jennings. However, what is striking in this description is that Jennings' hair is symbolic of duality. The description of Jennings' hair is significant because it shows how appearances are more important than personality in this novel. Jennings is Blake's double in the way that earlier on in his life; he had been 'accused of a crime that he did not commit' (p.208), but could not prove his innocence. Jennings presents what Blake might have become, if he could not clear his name. Thus, Jennings and Rosanna are two examples of society's unsympathetic attitudes towards those who are 'different', even if they are good people. Politically, opium is a substance used to say something about Britain's foreign policy at this time. Collins could have easily portrayed Blake sleepwalking without opium, but the fact that opium plays a role in this text exposes Britain's fallacy of adopting a free trade policy. The opium wars of 1839 and 1859-1860 were prompted by Britain's intervention in its trade policy, which led to the subsequent dispute regarding the purchase of tea, with Indian opium, which China forbade. Gail Marshall states:

---

[47] Gail Marshall, *Victorian Fiction* (London: Arnold Publishers, 2002), p.68.

> When the government intervened by going to war with China, they were in effect admitting that 'free trade' was unfeasible. (P.68)

The novel begins with the battle of Seringapatam (1799), a historical event which secured the power of the English East India Company in India. The English East India Company ensured England's presence and predominance in India throughout the nineteenth century. Collins's depiction of John Herncastle's unethical theft of the diamond from the castle of Seringapatam and the rightful restoration of the diamond to India is a critique of Britain's imperialism. In the prologue, John Herncastle is presented as a reclusive man. Instead of representing civilization, he represents materialism and murder:

> A cry inside hurried me into a room, which appeared to serve as an armoury. A third Indian, mortally wounded, was sinking at the feet of a man whose back was towards me. The man turned at the instant when I came in, and I saw John Herncastle, with a torch in one hand, and a dagger dripping with blood in the other. (P.5)

The fact that this is introduced to the reader at the beginning of the novel suggests that this novel is concerned with different systems of value. The difference between British and Indian ethics is brought into question in this novel: 'who is the civilized and who is the savage?' The Moonstone's entrance into various systems of value traces its trajectory through the novel. When the diamond is part of the Indian Moon god idol, it is spiritually valuable. When stolen by John Herncastle and willed to his niece, the diamond becomes valuable as an exotic heirloom, in other words it is so valuable that it is 'priceless' (p.168). It takes Godfrey Ablewhite and Septimus Luker to place the diamond into the market economy in order to receive money.

The text seems to suggest that the motive behind the imperial project is purely materialistic. Collins seems to alert to this notion on the evening of Rachel's birthday party. All of the English characters presume that the Indian men outside the house are jugglers: 'here were the jugglers returning to us' (p.78). The reality is that the jugglers are amateurs, but have come to England to claim the moonstone. Mr. Murthwaite discloses this information to Blake:

> Those three Indians are no more jugglers than you and I are…All you have seen to-night is a very bad and clumsy imitation of it… Those men are high caste Brahmins. (P.79)

This example is another instance of Britain's ignorance of India's culture. It takes Mr. Murthwaite an Indian, to tell Blake that 'there must be some very serious motive' behind the juggling masquerade. This re-emphasizes that Britain needs to understand India's culture, and not see it as a country for worldly gain.

Sleepwalking in *The Moonstone*, *Dracula* and "Who Killed Zebedee?" highlight the authors' apprehension of Britain as a nation and imperialist power. It is not only in novels that sleepwalking is related to the anxiety about state but also in film. The best example of this is Robert Wiene's film entitled *The Cabinet of Dr. Caligari*. Even though this film was produced in 1919, eighteen years outside the Victorian time frame, it is an important example that identifies sleepwalking with decline of Germany. The film presents the somnambulist Cesare, who is depicted as a menacing figure as he kills innocent victims. What makes this film distressing is that Cesare is hypnotised by Caligari in order to commit crime. The intention behind Caligari hypnotising Cesare is to show that the German war government seem to act as the prototype of voracious authority. The character of Caligari stands for unlimited authority that idolizes power and seeks only to control and dominate. Even though Cesare is a murderer, he is not really to blame for his actions because everything he does is controlled by Caligari, a figure of authority. Siegfried Kracauer agrees with this point by stating:

> Cesare is not so much a guilty murderer as caligari's innocent victim… According to the pacifist-minded Janowitz, they had created Cesare with the dim design of portraying the common man who, under the pressure of compulsory military service, is drilled to kill and to be killed.[48]

---

[48] Siegfried Kracauer, *From Caligari to Hitler: a psychological history of the German film* (Princeton: Princeton University Press, 1974), P.65.

The film is concerned with presenting the 'manifestations of a profoundly agitated soul/mind'. The film is an example of expressionist art which:

> Exposes the soul wavering between tyranny and chaos, and facing a desperate situation: any escape from tyranny seems to throw it into a state of utter confusion. (P.70)

The film expresses itself visually by using key props and visual devices to reinforce the theme of authority having unlimited power over the individual. For instance when the streets are presented, they are usually zigzags that run down them and up the walls. The use of the zigzags mirrors the distorted and chaotic mind of the individual and the state of post war Germany. Furthermore, the theme of tyranny pervades the screen from beginning to end by the use of Swivel-chairs which are of enormous height that symbolize the superiority of the city officials. The gigantic shadow of a chair in Alan's attic testifies to the invisible presence of powers that have their grip on him. Staircases reinforce this idea of hierarchy and power which are potent in the lunatic asylum. Three parallel flights of stairs are called upon to mark Dr. Caligari's position as the top of the hierarchy and his ability to control the common man. Rae Beth Gordon states:

> Psychotic and hysterical feelings and sensations are expressed through the décor of zigzags that run down streets and up walls, that constitute the contours of the houses and the fairground, that make up many of Caligari's gestures and corporeal poses, that are especially blatant in the outline of the rooftops over which the somnambulist carries the unconscious heroine[49]

Caligari's ability to hypnotize Cesare is a foreboding of the 'hypnotic effect Hitler produced on an audience'[50]. The anxiety about the relationship between leader and individual is examined in Gustave Le Bon's *Crowd*

---

[49] Rae Beth Gordon, *Why the French Love Jerry Lewis: from Cabaret to Early Cinema* (Stanford: Stanford University Press, 2001), p.142.
[50] Alan Bullock, *Hitler and Stalin: Parallel Lives* (London: Fontana Press, 1998), p.79.

Psychology. Le Bon shared a notable distrust of democratic politics in the period 1890-1914. Le Bon believed that the political system was being increasingly dominated by irrational and spontaneous collective mechanisms. Modern French society seemed to be entering the 'era of crowds'. 'Crowds', wrote Le Bon in the introduction to *Crowd Psychology*:

> Have always been important factors in the life of people, but this role have never been as important as today. The unconscious action of crowds substituting itself for the unconscious activity of individuals is one of the principal characteristics of the present age[51]

Le Bon's usage of the words 'unconscious action' and 'conscious activity' show how he uses hypnotic terminology to describe the relationship between leader and crowd. As the text progresses, the image of the leader as hypnotist becomes clear:

> Crowds are to some extent in the position of the sleeper whose reason, suspended for the time being, allows the arousing in his mind of images of extreme intensity which would quickly be dissipated could they be submitted to the action of reflection. (P.75)

In the same way the somnambulist has no conscious recollection of what s/he is doing, so does the individual who becomes part of the crowd, as his thoughts and feelings diminish and becomes one with the sentiments of the leader and crowd:

> In the life of the isolated individual it would be dangerous for him to gratify these instincts, while his absorption in an irresponsible crowd, in which in consequence he is assured of impunity, gives him entire liberty to follow them. (P.64)

The amalgamation of novels, film and non fiction works are fascinating because they all seem to be expressing the same theme and that is the anxiety about the self within an uncertain state. The moral

---

[51] Gustave Le Bon, *The Crowd: a study of the popular mind* (London: Fisher Unwin, 1896), p.1.

behind each of these works is that a weak individual and state is vulnerable to danger in the form of a threatening and tyrannous power. In *Dracula*, the decline of Britain is a reason why Dracula preys upon London. In *The Moonstone*, Britain's image as a civilized state is negated by Herncastle's plundering, hence causing chaos in the Verinder household. Likewise in "Who Killed Zebedee?" appearances are not what they seem to be. It is not Mr Deluc who should be distrusted, but Priscilla an English woman, who commits murder. The use of all these works has proved that sleepwalking is not simply connected with the self or home but it is a device that all these artists have used to voice their apprehension of Britain, France and Germany's future.

Conclusion

The significance of sleepwalking is that it exposes the inadequacies of society and state. The theme that has emerged from examining issues such as law, marriage, rape and elopement is that society is a place where double standards exist. The texts in chapter one seem to suggest that rigid laws are only applied to women, who are expected to be submissive to social convention. Social and moral codes to do not apply to men, which enables Alec to rape Tess, Zebedee to desert Priscilla and Stephen Guest to escape moral condemnation for his elopement with Maggie. Sleepwalking, or the reference to it, is not simply a physical act of a disturbed or repressed mind, but is an extension of a world outside the novel, where an individual's identity can be accepted in a world of otherness. If society is supposed to be the epitome of stability and security, it fails to offer protection and justice to Tess, Priscilla, Maggie, Valeria, Rachel and Rosanna. Furthermore, society does not allow women to be individuals, they have to observe social tradition, or risk being 'fallen' as discussed in *The Law and the Lady*.

From what has been discussed in Dracula, "Carmilla" and "Le Horla", the gothic and fantastic milieu is concerned with extremes and boundaries. The use of extremes in these texts suggest that individuals and society as a whole is unstable. Dracula's invasion into London and Le Horla's taunting of the narrator imply that people and society are vulnerable to other external forces, which are beyond one's control. However much society attempts to control individuals such as Lucy and Laura, it will fail because vampirism accepts them as individuals in its own world. The fact that Lucy and Laura are seduced into vampirism, reemphasizes the same argument in chapter one, which is society needs to revise its gender roles. The fact that Lucy seeks sanctuary in vampirism, suggests that society should not punish women for their desires, but should be treated as equals with men, who possess desire and seek love, as opposed to being the submissive wife and mother like Mina Harker.

Sleepwalking reveals the incompetence of Britain, France and Germany to offer stability to its citizens. Britain is portrayed as a materialistic country, that plunders the wealth of other countries in its empire as seen in *The Moonstone*. The suspicious outlook that Britons have of foreigners such as Ezra Jennings and Mr. Deluc exhibits Britain's prejudice towards those who appear to be 'different'. The irony in *The Moonstone* and "Who Killed Zebedee?" is that it is Priscilla, an English woman who murders Zebedee and John Herncastle a representative of the English army, who steals the moonstone, thus, causing chaos to the Verinder household. What is clear throughout this discussion is that the instability of the self is due to society and the state. Dracula is not the only monster invading society, but society itself is the monster within, controlling and punishing the individual.

Bibliography

Introduction:

Bullen, J.B. ed., *Writing and Victorianism* (London: Longman, 1997).
Dickens, Charles, *Oliver Twist* (London: Harmondsworth, 1985).
Small, Helen, and Trudi Tate, ed., *Literature, Science, and Psychoanalysis 1830-1970* (Oxford: Oxford University Press, 2003).
Taylor, Jenny Bourne, and Sally Shuttleworth, ed., *Embodied Selves: An Anthology of Psychological Texts 1830-1890* (Oxford: Clarendon Press, 1998).

"My dear John's dead murdered! I did it in my sleep": Sleepwalking & women:

Beer, Gillian, *George Eliot* (Indiana, Indiana University Press, 1986).
Bellini, Vincenzo, *La Sonnambula in full score* (Dover: Dover Publications, 2004).
Bellini, Vincenzo, *La Sonnambula* (Legaro Classics Archives, 1956).
Brady, Kristen, *George Eliot* (Basingstoke: Macmillan, 1992).
Clément, Catherine, *Opera, or the Undoing of Women,* trans. Betsy Wing (Minnesota: The University of Minnesota, 1988).
Collins, Wilkie, *The Law and the Lady* (Oxford: Oxford University Press, 1992).
Collins, Wilkie, *The Moonstone* (Oxford: Oxford University Press, 1982).
Collins, Wilkie, "Who Killed Zebedee?" (London: Hesperus Press Limited, 2002).

Davis, Lloyd, ed., *Virginal Sexuality and Texuality in Victorian Literature* (New York: State University of New York Press, 1993).

Eigen, Joel Peter, *Unconscious Crime: Mental Absence and Criminal Responsibility in Victorian London* (Baltimore: The John Hopkins University Press, 2003).

Eliot George, *The Mill on the Floss* (Oxford: Oxford University Press, 1985).

Foucault, Michel, *The History of Sexuality*, Vol.1, trans. Robert Hurley (New York: Vintage, 1980).

Hardy, Thomas, *Tess of the d'Urbervilles* (Oxford: Oxford University Press, 1983).

Heller, Tamar, *Dead Secret: Wilkie Collins and the Female Gothic* (New Haven: CT, 1992).

Irigaray, Lucy, *The Sex Which is Not One*, 1977, trans. Catherine Porter (Ithaca: NY, 1985)

Kristeva, Julia, *Powers of Horror* (New York: Columbia University Press, 1982).

Morgan, Rosemarie, *Women and Sexuality in the novels of Thomas Hardy* (London: Routledge, 1988).

Nunokawa, Jeff, 'Tess, tourism and the spectacle of the woman', in L.M.Shires, ed., *Rewriting the Victorians: Theory, History and the Politics of Gender* (London: Routledge, 1992).

Pall Mall Gazette, 50 (20.1.1890).

Priestman, Martin, ed., *The Cambridge Companion to Crime Fiction* (Cambridge: Cambridge University Press, 2003).

Pykett, Lyn, *The Sensation Novel: from The Woman In White to The Moonstone* (Plymouth: Northcote House, 1994).

Ruskin, John, *Sesame and Lilies: Two Lectures* (London: George Allen, 1901).

Samson, Jim, ed., *The Cambridge History of Nineteenth century Music* (Cambridge: Cambridge University Press, 2001).

Showalter, Elaine, *A literature of their own: from Charlotte Brontë to Dorris Lessing* (London: Virago, 1975).

Slung, Michele, *Crime on Her Mind* (New York: Harmondsworth, 1974).

Smart, Ann Mary, ed., *Siren Songs: Representations of Gender & Sexuality in Opera* (Princeton: Princeton University Press, 2000).

Strachey, James, ed., 'Dora' and 'Little Hans', trans. Alix & James Strachey (London: Penguin, 1990).

Taylor, Jenny Bourne, *In the Secret Theatre of Home: Wilkie Collins, Sensation Narrative and Nineteenth-Century Psychology* (London: Routledge, 1988).

Trodd, Anthea, *Domestic Crime in the Victorian Novel* (London: Longman, 1989).

Wright, Elizabeth, *Speaking desires can be dangerous: the poetics of the unconscious* (Cambridge: Cambridge University Press, 2003).

Weber, A.S., *19th Century Science: a selection of original texts* (Canada: Broadview, 2000).

'Who is he, this invisible being that rules me?' Sleepwalking/the gothic/the supernatural:

Benfield, Ben Barker, "The Spermatic Economy: A nineteenth century view of sexuality", *Feminist Studies 1*, (1972), 45-74.

Botting, Fred, "Aftergothic: consumption, machines and blackholes", in *The Cambridge Companion to Gothic Fiction*, ed. Jerrold E. Hogle (Cambridge: Cambridge University Press, 2002).

Bronfen, Elizabeth, *Over Her Dead Body: Death, Femininity and the Aesthetic* (Manchester: Manchester University press, 1975).

Brooke, Christine Rose, *rhetoric of the unreal: studies in the narrative and structure, especially of the fantastic* (Cambridge: Cambridge University Press, 1981).

Coleman, "The Phantom Double: its psychological significance", in *British Journal of Medical Psychology*, Vol. 14 (1934), 260-262, 272-273.

Copjec, Joan, "Vampires, Breast-feeding and Anxiety", in *Read my Desire: Lacan against the Historicists* (Cambridge, Mass.: MIT Press, 1994), 117-39.

Craft, Christopher, "'Kiss me with those red lips': Gender and Inversion in Bram Stoker's *Dracula*', in Carter (ed.), *Dracula: The Vampire and the critics*, 167-94.

Farson, Daniel, *The man who wrote Dracula: a biography of Bram Stoker* (London: Michael Joseph, 1975).

Foote, Edward Bliss, *Cyclopedia of Popular Medical, Social and Sexual Science* (London: L.N. Fowler, 1901).

Gelder, Ken, *Reading the Vampire* (London: Routledge, 1994).

Goldfarb, Russel, *Sexual Repression and Victorian Literature* (Bucknell: Bucknell University Press, 1975).

Hurley, Kelly, "British Gothic Fiction, 1885-1930", in *The Cambridge Companion to Gothic Fiction*, ed. Jerrold E. Hogle (Cambridge: Cambridge University Press, 2002).

Le Fanu, Sheridan, "Carmilla" (France: Zulma Classics, 2005).

Maupassant, Guy de, "Le Horla" (Paris: Libraire Générale Française, 1976).

Michie, Helen, *The Flesh Made Word: Female Figures and Women's Bodies* (Oxford: Oxford University Press, 1987).

Pope, Rebecca A., "Writing and Biting in Dracula", *LIT*, 1 (1990), 199-216.

Prichard, James Cowles, *Somnambulism and Animal Magnetism* (London, 1834).

Richardson, Maurice, 'The Psychoanalysis of Ghost Stories', *Twentieth Century*, 166 (December, 1959).

Sage, Victor, *Le Fanu's Gothic: the rhetoric of darkness* (Basingstoke: Macmillan, 2004).

Signorotti, Elizabeth, "Repossessing the body: transgressive desire in 'Carmilla' and Dracula". September 22, 1996. http://www.findarticles/lit/Elizabethsignorotti.

Spender, Dale, *Man Made Language* (London: Faber, 1985).

Stoker, Bram, *Dracula* (Oxford: Oxford University Press, 1998).

Todorov, Tzvetan, *The Fantastic: a structural approach to a literary genre* (Ithaca: Cornell University Press, 1975).

'Britain is sleepwalking into hell's pit': Sleepwalking & the state:

Bullock, Alan, *Hitler and Stalin: Parallel Lives* (London: Fontana Press, 1998).

Byron, Glennis, ed., *Dracula* (Basingstoke: Macmillan, 1999).

David, Deirdre, ed., *The Cambridge Companion to the Victorian Novel* (Cambridge: Cambridge University Press, 2001).

Doyle, Arthur Conan, *A Study in Scarlet* (Oxford: Oxford University Press, 1993).

Gordon, Rae Beth, *Why the French love Jerry Lewis: from cabaret to early cinema* (Stanford: Stanford University Press, 2001).

Hayter, A., *Opium and the Romantic Imagination* (London: Faber, 1968).

Hughes, William, *Beyond Dracula: Bram Stoker's fiction and its cultural context* (Basingstoke: Macmillan, 2000).

Kennedy, Paul, *The Rise and Fall of the Great Powers: economic change and military conflict from c.1500-c.2000* (New York: Random House, 1987).

Kracauer, Siegfried, *From Caligari to Hitler: A psychological history of the German film* (Princeton: Princeton University press, 1974).

Le Bon, Gustave, *Crowd Psychology* (London: Fisher Unwin, 1896).

Linton, Elizabeth Lynn, "The girl of the period", in *The Girl of the Period and other Social Essays*, Vol. 1. (London: Bentley, 1883), P.1.

Marshall, Gail, *Victorian Fiction* (London: Arnold Publishers, 2002).

Nye, Robert A., *The Origins of Crowd Psychology* (London: SAGE Publications, 1975).

Pick, Daniel, *Faces of Degeneration: A European Disorder Cc. 1848-c.1918* (Cambridge: Cambridge University Press, 1989).

Porter, Bernard, *The absent-minded imperialists: empire, society and culture in Britain* (Oxford: Oxford University Press, 2004).

Said, Edward, *Orientalism* (London: Routledge, 1978).

Smith, Andrew, and William Hughes, ed., *Empire and Gothic: the politics of genre* (Basingstoke: Macmillan, 2003).

Stead, W.T. http://www.alangullette.com/lit/shiel/essays/shiel_stead.htm.

The Lancet, "Are we degenerating physically?", Vol. 2 (1888), 1,076.

Thompson, Andrew Stuart, *Imperial Britain: The empire in British politics c.1880-c.1932* (London: Longman, 2000).

Wiene, Robert, *The Cabinet of Dr. Caligari* (London: Redemption Films, 1919).